Hisss

SKYE MACKINNON

CONTENTS

A quick word before we get started   v
What Happened Before   vii

Prologue   1
Chapter 1   5
Chapter 2   15
Chapter 3   22
Chapter 4   29
Chapter 5   39
Chapter 6   46
Chapter 7   53
Chapter 8   67
Chapter 9   76
Chapter 10   87
Chapter 11   99
Chapter 12   109
Chapter 13   117
Chapter 14   128
Chapter 15   136
Chapter 16   144
Chapter 17   155
Chapter 18   163
Chapter 19   174
Chapter 20   180
Chapter 21   187
Epilogue   196

Author's Note   201
About the Author   203

Hisss © Copyright 2019 Skye MacKinnon

All rights reserved under the International and Pan-American Copyright Conventions. No part of this book may be reproduced or transmitted in any form or by any means, electronic or mechanical, including photocopying, recording, or by any information storage and retrieval system, without permission in writing from the publisher.

This is a work of fiction. Names, places, characters and incidents are either the product of the author's imagination or are used fictitiously, and any resemblance to any actual persons, living or dead, organizations, events or locales is entirely coincidental.

Cover by Ravenborn Covers.

Formatting by Gina Wynn.

skyemackinnon.com

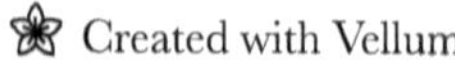 Created with Vellum

A QUICK WORD BEFORE WE GET STARTED

As you will know from the previous three books, this series is set in a world very similar to our own, but there are some deciding differences. Technology has developed differently, and while there are many devices you may be used to, such as televisions, there are no mobile phones, cars or the internet. No guns, either.

This book is written in British English and uses some British expressions and idioms. Please don't see these as spelling mistakes. We say mum rather than mom, use a lot of 's' instead of 'z' (cosy, realise, …) and use 'got' as the past participle of 'get' (instead of 'gotten').

And finally, subscribe to Skye's newsletter for updates about new releases: skyemackinnon.com/newsletter.

You'll even get a free book for subscribing, so it's totally worth it.

Kat is an assassin who runs M.E.O.W. together with her friends Lily (half-succubus), Bethany (poisons expert) and Benjamin (thief). While solving the murder of a sweetshop owner, she met her old friend Lennox (a wolf shifter) as well as the mysterious Gryphon, who later turns out to be a siren. That's important because his kind secretly runs not only the city, but also the Pack, the assassin mafia Kat grew up in. While trying to find out who's behind the murder, Kat and her team stumble across the Fangs, a crime organisation who may just control the entire country, even though very few people have ever heard of them.

Kat has the ingenious idea of employing the local cat population to help her solve crimes and spy on people. The cats are led by the majestic Ryker, who turns out to be a cat shifter himself. Slowly, she gets closer to Ryker, once he finally learns to shift into a human, but he's not the only one. Lennox's wolf claims Kat as his mate and Gryphon seduces her with his siren magic. Suddenly, she's got three men vying for her attention while she also tries to understand her past.

She grew up in the Pack where she was forced to become an assassin, mistreated and controlled with a collar. Kat always thought her mother abandoned her there, but now she's told she's actually a clone, one of eight, and the woman she thought was her mother was the original template. Kat kills the woman who created her, Jacqueline Fitzroy (aka Grandma Doctor), and sets the laboratory on fire. She gets a little hurt, but oh well, she heals and can soon speak human again too.

From the files they took from the lab, they discover that there were fifty-three clone embryos, but only ten survived past the age of one (yes, Fitzroy lied about that). The aim of the cloning was to produce an obedient but lethal cat shifter who didn't need to be collared to be controlled. A drug was given to all the clones and Bethany tries to figure out what it did. Maybe it has something to do with the memories that Kat seems to be missing... The other scientist who worked on the project, Professor Lakefield, turns out to be Kat's mysterious benefactor who'd freed her of her collar – it was all a lie, just another experiment.

Kat takes in one of the clones, Little Kat, but that means eight other clones are still somewhere out there, unless they have perished in the meantime.

The Pack retaliates for M.E.O.W. destroying their lab by kidnapping Benjamin and Gryphon. They've created a new kind of shifter hybrid, who can heal extremely fast. Kat manages to kill some of them, but eventually, Ryker and her get captured. Tortured and starved, Kat escapes, stronger than ever before. Her feral side takes over and she goes on a killing spree until she manages to free Ryker. Gryphon is missing though and she traces him to the Pack, where he's walking around a free man. Has he betrayed them? Kat confronts him and she's taken to the Pack's leaders in a collar. It's all a ruse though and together, Kat and Gryphon kill them all.

Sadly, the Pack destroyed their M.E.O.W. headquarters, so they're now living in a wagon. They lost all their belongings, including the research they'd recovered from the Pack labs, so they still don't have all the answers. At the end of Purrr, two clones appear on Kat's doorstep… let's continue the story there.

They made us at the same time. Like twins.

We're the same.

Completely.

I know what she thinks…

…before I do. And I laugh about her jokes…

…before I've completed my sentence.

We're the same.

That's why they created us together.

They wanted to see how similar we would be if we grew up in the same surroundings.

But they didn't expect us to be this close.

The original was antisocial. They thought we'd dislike each other.

Instead, we became one.

Being apart was…is terrible.

It was an experiment. Separate us and have us in different cities.

So far away from each other.

But I felt her.

I kept hearing her thoughts.

And we made plans to escape.

They never knew we could communicate over distances.

We made sure they didn't know that.

After we escaped, we found each other again.

We're more than the sum of our parts.

So much more.

We knew there were others, but we couldn't hear them like we can hear each other.

We searched for them. Found one, but it was too late.

She was too young to die. They'll pay.

Yes, they will pay.

Now we've found another.

The first of us. The oldest.

She's started the battle here in the city where we were created

but she doesn't know the full picture. She's not realised yet

how deep the roots have spread.

We're going to have to tell her or it might be too late.

She has others with her. They might distract her.

She's the priority. If they get in the way of our plans…

…we'll dispose of them.

CHAPTER ONE

The two girls sit on the sofa, their thighs touching, their hands entwined. It's like I'm seeing myself in a mirror from six years ago. Plus double vision. It's slightly disconcerting how alike they look. Not just like each other, but also like me.

My sisters. They've introduced themselves as Four and Five, although Five goes by Ivy. They've not really said anything else, and I've been too busy staring at them to start a conversation. Everyone else is doing the same, staring, looking startled and confused.

Nobody expected any of the clones to find *us*.

"Nice wagon," Ivy says eventually. Even her voice is exactly like mine, although she has a slight accent I can't quite place.

"It's only temporary," I say, distracted by the whole situation. "Our house was set on fire."

"The Pack?" Four asks, and I nod.

"They didn't like us torching their labs."

The two girls exchange a look and grin. "We

thought that may have been you," Ivy says with a smile. "We knew about you, but because you were working with Lakefield, we weren't sure what side you were on."

Lakefield. Mystery Man. I'm still not over that betrayal. The man I thought I could trust, who I believed had saved me from the Pack, had actually been one of my creators.

"Don't worry, he's dead," I spit. "I definitely wasn't working with him. He deceived me."

Four nods. "He does that. Did. It was good to hear of his death."

"You two seem very well informed," Gryphon remarks. He's sitting on top of the kitchen cupboard, his long legs dangling.

"We need to be," the two say as one. Okay, now that's really creepy.

"We escaped two years ago," Four explains. "We've been running ever since. Knowing what our enemies are up to has kept us alive."

"We've wanted to kill him for ages," Ivy adds. "But that would have meant going out in the open and we weren't ready for that yet. Now, we are. We've trained, we've gathered as much intel as we can. We're ready to fight."

There was only one mention of twins in the clone files, and according to those, these two girls are only about fourteen years old. They behave like they're older than me, in a way. Creeeeepy. They're my sisters and I should probably feel some kind of instant connection with them, but for now, I'm hesitant in opening up to them. It could be a trick. They could easily still be in the hands of the Pack. K4 and K5, that means there were two other clones in between them and me. Many opportunities for the Pack scientists to perfect their methods, to make the clones more obedient. It could all be yet another trap and I'm not going to spring it.

Lily studies them curiously. "How do I tell you apart? Do you have different birthmarks or something like that?"

The girls smirk, exchanging another mirthful look.

"You can't," Four says with a wide grin. "When we were at the Pack, they put numbers on our shirt and made us have our hair at different lengths. Now, we're taking advantage of being twins. Nobody can tell us apart."

I stay quiet. I think I can already. Not by looks but by scent. They smell incredibly similar, but Ivy's scent is a tiny bit sweeter.

"Do you live here in town?" Bethany asks. I'm grateful my team are doing the interrogation. I'm way too confused to do much more than stare and listen.

Four nods. "We returned three months ago. When we first escaped, we ran as far as we could, but we got tired of behaving like prey. We decided it was time to come back and do some damage. Hunt the people who did this to us."

"Did what?" Bethany leans forwards, her hands clasped beneath her chin. She reminds me of a detective questioning her suspects, but she's the good cop, the friendly one. It's completely the opposite of her usual grumpy, bored manner.

The twins look straight at me. "The memories," Ivy

says with a slight grimace. "Do you have any missing, Kat?"

It's the first time they've used my name. A shiver runs down my back. It feels wrong to have a version of myself say my name without it belonging to them.

"It's not like I miss them," I say hesitantly. "I didn't know any were missing at all until that doctor told me I'd seen him before yet I couldn't remember. He showed me pictures of people I ought to recognise, but I just drew blanks. But it's strange, I don't *feel* like I forgot something, if you know what I mean."

"You can't remember that you can't remember," Four mutters softly. "Right?"

I nod. "Exactly that. It's the same for you?"

"Yes, but I have less missing than Ivy. She-"

"I can't remember the first seven years of my life," Ivy interrupts. "That's what they did to me. They took my memories without bothering to replace them. I know they're missing because for me, it feels like a gaping black hole within my mind. Four has told me what happened back then, yet even knowing, I can't remember. It's just gone, all of it." She swallows visibly. "I want them back."

Four squeezes her sister's hand. "And we're going to get them. Somehow."

Gryphon clears his throat. "Girls, I'm sorry to say this, but we kind of torched the Pack labs plus killed a lot of people working there."

"We know," Ivy snaps. "But you didn't destroy all of them."

I sit up straight. "There's more?"

She nods. "We know of at least one other lab. We've not been strong enough yet to go there, but with you on our side, it should be safe enough. She's a bitch, but even she can be overwhelmed by three of us."

"She?" I ask, alarm bells ringing in my head.

The twins look at each other. "She doesn't know," Ivy whispers, her eyes wide.

Ominous much?

"How many of us do you know about?" Four asks me cautiously.

"Little Kat, that's K8, and now the two of you. We were going to look for the others, but the Pack destroyed my headquarters and we lost most of our intel. We're going to have to start from scratch again."

The girls exchange another look. I wish they'd stop doing that. It makes me feel stupid, like I only have half the puzzle pieces and they're refusing to give me the rest of them.

"We thought you'd know more by now," Ivy says, almost accusingly. "You've been here while we were out of town. You had all the advantage."

"I've been out of the Pack's clutches for only a few months-" I swallow hard. No, that's wrong. "Days," I correct myself. "I thought I was free, yet they've been monitoring me the entire time. Until we broke into the lab, I didn't even know I was a clone, nor that there were others. I'm still catching up."

"We know." Ivy rolls her eyes. "That's why we didn't contact you until now. We had to wait until you were truly free."

I stare at her. "So you could have contacted me before? Told me that the Pack was watching me?"

She shrugs. "Yes, but we were busy hunting for the others. We knew where you were and that you were fighting on our side, more or less. It's all about priorities."

They're only supposed to be fourteen, right? Yet they're so jaded that they seem a lot older.

"How many do you know of?" I ask her.

"You, K2 and K7. K3 and K6 are dead. You said you know K8, so that only leaves the youngest ones."

She doesn't even blink when she says that two of us have died. K3. K6. Did they ever have a real name? Did they ever get a taste of freedom? I decide not to ask. This isn't the time to dwell on the past. Once we've razed the Pack to the ground, I'm going to mourn her. Until then, I need to focus on the present.

"We don't know how many there are," Four adds. "Do you?"

"Doctor Fitzroy told me seven, but then we found files mentioning ten...clones. Maybe there are even more, but let's assume ten at the very least. That means K9 and K10 may still be out there. Who's K7?"

"She's...different," Ivy says hesitantly. "She's still with them. We weren't sure we could take care of her if we freed her."

"Different how?" Bethany asks, taking the words right out of my mouth.

"It's hard to describe. One moment she's a normal child, the next she's rabid, feral. They didn't put a collar on her, so we think they did something to her that made her this way."

I shudder at the thought. Yet another one of us whose future they destroyed.

"Where is she now?"

"Attenburgh. They don't call themselves the Pack there, but they're the same, more or less."

"I know the people in charge there," Gryphon hisses. "They're the worst. Even my father tried not to do business with them if he could avoid it."

Sirens that other sirens were afraid of. That was bad.

"We'll have to get her out of there eventually," I say, pushing down the tremble that's trying to sneak into my voice. "And destroy the people keeping her captive. We need to make sure nobody ever gets the chance to do this to others. Let us be the last ones."

Four nods. "Are you aware of the Fangs?"

"Unfortunately."

She grimaces. "Yeah, I know what you mean. We only found out about them recently, but it's clear that it's them pulling the strings. And even if we eradicate the Pack here and in Attenburgh, they might still have the information on how to do the cloning. We need to go all the way to the top."

"That's impossible," Beth interjects. "Nobody knows who the Fangs are. They hide in plain sight and it's said that they're everywhere. For all we know, they're spread all over the country. We could never kill them all, as much as I would like to."

"No, but maybe there's another way," Gryphon says

slowly. "We could try and infiltrate them. Gather information from the inside before we strike."

Ivy laughs. "And then we'll all ride on unicorns." She turns to me. "Your team reflects badly on you."

"No, it doesn't. Show them, Gryphon."

"With pleasure."

He gets up and clears his throat. Knowing what's about to come, I steel my mind. I don't want to fall under his spell and start kissing him again. Or stabbing him like the first time showed me his siren powers.

Gryphon opens his mouth and begins to sing. Music chimes in my head, not just the siren's voice, but an entire orchestra. I close my eyes and let the beautiful sounds wash over me. I relax for the first time in days. I'm safe. Loved. Happy. I don't resist the music. I could, but I don't want to. I soak it in like a drug. Happiness is sparse right now and this is a chance to feel *good*.

Images appear in my mind. Gryphon, smiling at me. Dimples line his lips. His eyes full of warmth. A kiss, soft yet claiming. Me in his arms. The love in his touch as his hands roam across my body.

The music stops without warning and I open my eyes. Everyone is looking dazed but happy, except for Four. She's on Gryphon's lap, her hand at his throat, her claws extended. Fuck.

She turns to me, her face contorted with fury. "You let one of *them* into your house?!"

I get up and calmly put a hand on hers, pulling her away from Gryphon. She lets me, luckily. I don't want to fight one of my sisters.

"He's not like the rest of his kind," I explain gently.

I'm still in a happy, calm mood; otherwise I would have probably reacted very differently to her threatening one of my guys. "He's on our side, and he's proved it. I trust him implicitly."

She stares at me defiantly. "You can't be serious. He's enchanted you."

Gryphon chuckles. "It's her who's enchanted me."

"Not the time," Ryker groans "Stop flirting with Kat."

Ivy looks around the room. "You're all okay with him being here? You all trust him?"

My team nod as one. I smile at them. "See? He's part of M.E.O.W. We can't choose our family nor our upbringing. The three of us should know that better than anyone."

Four wriggles out of my grasp and joins her sister on the bench. "What does M.E.O.W. stand for, anyway?" she asks.

I let her change the topic. For now. If she attacks Gryphon again, I'm not going to be so lenient.

Lily snickers. "We don't know."

"How can you not know?" Ivy asks, incredulous. "Who came up with the name?"

I raise my hand, grinning. "I just added the dots to make it look more professional. The original idea was just to call it 'Meow'. The sound I make when I kill someone. We've come up with a few versions since then, but none of them has stuck."

"Such as?"

"Murder, Eviscerations, Obliterations, Wounds," Benjamin supplies. "That's my favourite version."

"Men endanger our world," Lily chuckles.

"Oi!" Benjamin waves his hands at her.

She laughs dismissively. "You're not a man. You're a boy."

Bethany clears her throat. "My Eyes On Wealth. Or Willies, if we're talking about Lily."

"Oi! I've not done any seducing in ages." Lily rolls her eyes. "Been too busy playing with pussies."

The twins stare at us. "You're weird," Four says.

I laugh and my friends join me. Yes, we are. But we're M.E.O.W. *Murder, every one wants.*

CHAPTER TWO

The wagon really isn't big enough for us. Lily and Bethany share one small bedroom at the other end, Benjamin is sleeping on the bench in the kitchen and I'm crammed in between Ryker, Gryphon and Lennox on our giant mattress. We need to get ourselves a proper house again, but right now, it's not worth settling somewhere before we know what's going to happen next. This wagon is portable. If we get some horses, we can use it to travel to Attenburgh or some other town we need to go to.

The twins have left. They refused to tell me where they're staying and only said they'd be back tomorrow. I get why they don't trust me. I don't trust them either, yet. We might be the same physically, but who knows what goes on in their heads. If they're anything like me, they know how to lie and deceive. That's the scary bit. I don't want them to be that jaded, but after talking to them, they might be even more broken than I am.

Ryker slides an arm underneath my shoulders and

pulls me closer. I give in and snuggle against him. Lennox growls in protest and shuffles close to me from the other side. Gryphon is already fast asleep next to Ryker; otherwise he'd probably try and join the cuddle party.

I never used to like being in a bed with a man after shagging him. I had sex because I have urges, because it was fun, but I didn't really care about the man attached to the cock in me. Now, I have three men in my bed and I don't want to kick them out. How quickly things can change.

Now that I'm no longer in heat, I don't feel like I have to screw the guys. I'm content just snuggling with them, enjoying their closeness. Yup, I've changed. I'm losing my edge. If I had any sense of self-preservation left, I'd run now before I get even more attached.

"Don't," Lennox whispers.

"Huh?"

"I know what you're thinking. You're scared of being happy. You want to run. You don't want us to get too close. You're worried we'll break through the walls you've built around yourself."

"You're wrong," I mutter, even though he's hit the nail on the head.

"Is he?" Ryker asks softly. "Are you sure?"

"Don't you get involved as well. It's bad enough when the doggo starts going all emotional."

Lennox growls. "Who are you calling a dog?" With a speed that must have been increased by his shifter abilities, he rolls on top of me and pins me down. I struggle, but not as much as I should. If I wanted, I could get away from him, but I want to see what he does. Call it professional curiosity.

My pulse is speeding up and for once, I'm unable to control it. These boys are going to be the death of me. If they break through my walls, my protection, then I might not be strong enough to deal with the Pack. I need to prevent that. Saving my sisters is more important than my own happiness.

Lennox bends down, but just before his lips touch mine, I buckle and throw him off. And across the bed. He lands with his back against the wall, staring at me in surprise. Oops. I'm not used to my new strength yet. Whatever happened in the blue house with Boris the scientist, my body is a lot stronger now. Raw power is pulsing within me, wanting out. I'm no longer tired.

"Kat?" Gryphon sits up, rubbing his eyes. "What's going on?"

The worry in his gaze makes me want to puke. I scramble to my feet and run out of the room. Through the kitchen and out of the wagon I run until cold night air hits my face. I close the door behind me, making sure nobody is following me. I breathe in deep and look at the starry sky. With the wagon parked at the very outskirts of the town, we're far from any light pollution. I never got to see this many stars from the M.E.O.W. headquarters.

Footsteps inside the wagon tell me that I won't stay alone for long. Fuck. Why can't they leave me alone?

I take another deep breath and shift. It feels like I'm letting go of a mask and putting on my true skin. I hadn't realised how much effort it had been to stay human. I've not had time yet to figure out what happened to me in that lab, but I'm starting to think that I really need to do that soon. I'm stronger, but I'm also more feral. I keep having to control my feline temper.

After Mystery Man – no, Professor Lakefield – had taken off my collar, it took me weeks to get used to the feeling of no longer being caged. The feeling of freedom. Now, it seems like I've got to go through a similar process all over again.

I pounce and run. Instead of taking to the roofs of the town like I usually do, I turn the other direction, away from the houses and towards the fields and forests. Tonight, I feel like I need to breathe. I need space, not the confinements of town.

I race across the uneven ground, revelling in the way my body moves. Muscles stretch and relax, stretch and relax. Wind strokes my black fur that makes me one with the night. I'm a lethal killing machine, built for strength and violence. Tonight though, I'm not going to kill. I'm just going to run and run until I'm tired.

Morning sun kisses my face.

No, wait. It's a kitten.

She licks my nose with her rough tongue. Weirdo.

I growl and she backs off a little, but doesn't seem scared in the slightest. Most kittens would be frightened of a massive panther, but not this one. I've not seen her around, but she smells like one of Ryker's clowder. He's taken in not only the kittens that Benjamin had been looking after in our house, but also some new strays. It seems he can't help himself. His heart is way too soft.

"Go away," I groan and put a paw across my eyes. It's not that I'm still tired, I just want to be alone for a little while longer. I can already feel that it's going to be a day where I don't want to be around anyone, neither cats nor humans. I think I've been surrounded by people far too much recently. My feline side doesn't like it.

She doesn't listen and lies down on the wet grass, snuggling against my side. Seriously? Have I lost my intimidating vibe now too?

"Fuck off," I snarl.

"Bad language," she mutters in a high, childish voice. "Ryker says we need to talk proper."

"Well, Ryker can kiss my furry arse."

"Why would he want to do that?"

I've never been so tempted to eat a kitten.

I sigh and glare at her. "What are you doing here? I'm busy."

"He told me to find you and make sure you were alright."

"Well, you've found me. Now go away."

The kitten gave me a disconcerting frown. Were cats supposed to have that much control over their forehead muscles?

"You're not very nice, you know?"

"Piss off."

Finally, she gets the message and walks away. I'd love to sleep some more, but thanks to that evil fluffball, I'm wide awake. I hate cats, and yes, I'm allowed to say that because I am one.

My stomach growls, telling me it's time to leave. Maybe I should have had the kitten for breakfast. Just kidding. I'm not into cannibalism. I get up and look around. I ran far last night, further than I've gone in ages. It'll take me a while to get back to the town. Annoyingly, that gives me more time to think. I did a lot of that yesterday. Now I just want to get on with life. Find my sisters. Create us a new home. Be happy. And yes, eventually I might be able to decide what to do about the guys too. Not now, though. The thought of analysing the way I react to them gives me the urge to cough up hairballs.

I sate my thirst at a small stream separating two lavender fields before making my way home in a gentle trot. It's a beautiful day, with sunlight warming my fur and butterflies bumping into my face, but I don't feel as happy as I perhaps should. I'm alive, all my friends are alive, yet there's a pit in my stomach that grows the closer I get to the town. I wish I knew what was wrong with me.

If I still had our old house, I'd sneak into the kitchen and indulge in some catnip. That always makes the world seem so much better. Catnip for the win. I doubt any of it survived the blaze though. I need to get more soon, for these dark moments when I need a little boost. Maybe Ryker has some, but that would mean being in his debt. No, I'll contact my usual suppliers, even if that takes a little longer.

I have to cross a narrow river before reaching the outskirts. There's a bridge, but people would see me, now that I no longer have the cover of darkness. I look at the cold, fast water. It's not just house cats who don't like water. I despise it too. I dip one paw into the river. Icy. Yuck. Perhaps this is a sign to stay on my own for a while longer. Not return to the others, just roam the wilds as a panther, live off the land, ignore my human problems. Oh, if life only were that simple.

Just when I'm about to gather my courage to leap into the water, a faint meow makes me turn towards the sound. I know that voice; it's the little kitten who woke me. She's in pain and she's scared. Fuck. Guess it's time to play saviour once again.

I follow her pitiful meows, away from the river and towards a small forest. Why the heck did the kitten even go here? It's not the direct way to the town and definitely not a shortcut.

When I get closer, a new scent hits my nostrils. Wet dog. No, not dogs. Wolves. Like Lennox's scent, but a lot more menacing. There are shifters out here and they're not the nice kind. This is getting ever more intriguing. Judging from the scents, there are at least three werewolves out here. If they're all the size of Lennox, that could be a bit of a challenge. Luckily, most wolf shifters are smaller than him and less powerful. There's no way around it, anyway. The kitten is in danger and I'm the only one around to help it.

Why can't people get themselves into trouble when I'm not nearby? That would be so much easier for me. Not for them, but still… sometimes I deserve to be selfish.

The forest gives me enough cover to slowly sneak up

on the wolves. I was right, there are three of them, surrounding the little kitten. She's got scratch wounds all over her little body, but they don't seem deep enough to be life-threatening. They're playing with her.

Anger fills me. I like torture as much as the next assassin, but I only do it to people who deserve it, not to innocent kittens. She's got her paws above her head, shielding herself from the next attack.

No more.

I leap out of the foliage and land on one of the wolves, pinning him to the ground. By the time the other two realise what's happening and turn towards me, I've already ripped out this one's throat. Blood fills my mouth, hot and sweet. I freeze, realising I shouldn't find it this...delicious. I shouldn't want to drink my fill from his bleeding throat.

One of the other wolves, a dark grey one, pounces and I react by instinct, rolling onto my side, evading him easily. The other joins the fray and then we're fighting, biting, clawing at each other. Every time I bite one of them, their blood joins that of the first in my mouth. I swallow it down, greedily drinking their life essence. The frenzy makes it hard to think, so I give my instincts free rein, fighting wild and dirty.

When one of them jumps into the air to attack me from above, I roll onto my back and extend my paws, slicing open his abdomen. Entrails rain down on me and all I can think of is how good they might taste. Hunger burns through me, a deep craving that won't be controlled. The wolf's body falls on top of me like a flying buffet. I open my jaws wide, catching whatever organs are tumbling towards me, but then the other wolf is there, his teeth sinking into my side.

I roar and roll to my feet, facing the ashen wolf who's growling at me. In slow motion, I see his hind legs lower, readying for the jump, but I'm faster. Before he's even left the ground, I'm on him, my claws racing across his back, my teeth at his neck. He's dead before he can take another breath.

Alright, this has never happened before. I'm fast, but not that fast. The wound in my side is throbbing, but the pain is already lessening. As if I'm healing at record speed.

The kitten meows pitifully. She licks blood off her little paws before progressing to the wounds she can reach. She seems fine though. A little shaken, a little bit injured, but nothing dramatic.

I turn away from her to focus on the wolf corpses. They smell delicious. Sweet, raw, with an echo of life. I want to sink my teeth into their flesh and rip them apart, wolfing down the fresh meat. Drink their blood.

"Please don't eat me."

The kitten's trembling words pull me from my frenzy.

I stare at her in shock. Blood is dripping from my fur, coating the inside of my mouth, filling my stomach. What the fuck have I done?

I stumble back, away from the corpses. Even though my head is slowly getting clearer, their scent is still tempting me. This is so much more potent than catnip. If the kitten weren't watching me with wide eyes, I'd devour them all until only bones are left.

"I'm not going to eat you," I mutter, retreating further. "How badly are you hurt?"

"I'll be fine," she says bravely, but her voice is weak.

I sigh and lower myself to the ground. "Climb on. I'll carry you."

She looks at me with fear reflecting in her large eyes. She's afraid of me, one of her own. I've really messed up.

"Do it now or you'll have to walk home," I snap, more harshly than I want to.

With another cautious glance, she does as I said, climbing onto my back, her little claws pressing against my skin as she finds a secure spot to hold on to. I carefully get up, making sure she's not about to slip. When I'm sure that she's safe up there, I increase my pace, hurrying towards town. As much as I want more solitude to think about what just happened, I've got a kitten in need of help.

BY THE TIME WE ARRIVE BACK AT THE WAGON, THE midday sun is burning down hard. The blood on my fur has dried and little flakes of it fall to the ground, leaving a bread crumb trail behind us. The kitten is holding on, but her grip is getting looser. She's not going to last for much longer.

Ryker's scent hits my nose moments before I can see him running towards us, shifted into his beautiful feline form. And then I'm surrounded by cats, a dozen of them, circling me like prey. I lower myself to the ground to let the kitten climb off, but she clings to me.

"Get off," I tell her, not unkindly. "Ryker can look after you now."

"Who's going to look after you?" she whispers with the tiniest of meows.

I laugh. "I can look after myself just fine. Come on, get off me or I'll have to make you."

Finally, she climbs down and is welcomed by her fellow cats. One large female starts licking the kitten. She doesn't smell like the little one's mother, but I'm glad there's someone taking care of the kitten. I realise I never even asked for her name. Oh well, I'm a cat, I'm not supposed to have social skills.

Ryker approaches me slowly and he stops a few feet away from me. His tail swings from side to side; he's nervous.

"What happened?" he asks, his eyes on the kitten rather than me. He's avoiding me. Is it the blood?

"Three wolves attacked her. Wolf *shifters*."

"Shifters?" He finally looks at me. "From the Pack?"

I shake my head. Blood flakes rain to the ground. I want to lick them up. "No, they didn't smell like the Pack. And…I think they were different. Remember the grunts at the blue house, the ones who didn't want to die?"

He nods, a pained expression flicking over his face. "Hard to forget them."

"They had a similar scent. And their blood tasted the same. Sweet. Like honey and milk."

"You drank their *blood?*" he asks, once again avoiding my eyes. Something is off between us.

"I ripped out their throats, so it kind of happened by accident. It's very hard not to get blood into your oesophagus when your jaws are clamped around a bleeding wound."

He nods, but the atmosphere isn't getting any more comfortable. I don't like what he's making me feel. Like I did something wrong.

"Tiny's going to be fine," the older cat interrupts. "I'm going to take her home."

Tiny must be the kitten's name. Very appropriate.

She gives me a little smile before walking away with the female. Some of the other cats follow them, but a few remain with Ryker and me. I wish they'd go. I don't like having an audience.

I nod towards the wagon. "Are the others inside?"

"Only Lennox and some of the humans. The twins left when you weren't there, and Gryphon said he had to attend to some business."

His words are harsh. He blames me for running away, for not staying with them. How can I explain that I'm not ready to be that close to people? I'm a cat, I'm not made for relationships. Ryker of all should know that, but it seems he's more human than I am, even though he grew up as a cat. How ironic.

I sigh. "If you have something to say, do it. But let's have some privacy." I glare at the cats surrounding us. I recognise a few of them, but even so, I don't want them to listen to this.

"No, I don't have anything to say. But we should go

and find out more about the wolves. If there are new predators nearby, I need to know about it." He turns to one of the male cats, a large tabby with a missing ear. "Greg, tell everyone to stay within the town. Nobody's to roam around until we know if there's more of them."

The tabby bows his head and runs off. The other cats follow him, finally leaving us alone.

"Ryker, I-"

"Maybe we should take Lennox with us," he interrupts. "In fact, shift and tell him what's happened. Then clean yourself up. We can follow your trail, we don't need you to come with us."

His words hurt more than the wound from earlier. The *normal* Kat would rise up, fight, argue, but I'm not feeling myself just now. I give off a light growl, just for the sake of it, and head towards the wagon. Dried blood still cakes my fur and I can't wait to get rid of it. Not because it makes me dirty. Because I want to lick it.

CHAPTER FOUR

Shifting got rid of most of the blood, but I take a shower nonetheless. The wagon's tiny bathroom makes me miss my old house with its massive shower and bathtub. Here, whenever I turn, I bump against the tiled walls. The water isn't very hot either. We really need to find ourselves a new home. I never realised how spoilt I'd become by having my own house. Back at the Pack, I slept in a dormitory and used a communal washroom. The wagon is a hundred times better than that. Still...once we've found all my sisters, I'll get us a new house. Luckily, we still have our bank accounts, and our little safe survived the fire, giving us enough cash to get by for a while.

I switch off the shower even though I don't feel completely clean yet. That's just a trick of my mind though, I know that. My body is clean; there isn't a drop of blood anywhere. It's all just in my head.

My stomach growls. It's time to check what was in the fridge.

Nothing. Well, two eggs and a sorry looking cabbage, but I'm on the hunt for meat. Or catnip, either would work.

"There's nothing in there, I already checked."

Benjamin stumbles into the kitchen, a scarf wound around his throat. He looks dreadfully pale.

"You alright?"

He shakes his head. "I think I've got a cold. Beth is off to the pharmacy to get some drugs. It turns out she's got a lot of poisons, but not much to heal people." He rolls his eyes. "I don't suppose you feel like going shopping?"

"I'm the leader of M.E.O.W. I don't go shopping. I have food delivered," I say haughtily.

Benjamin laughs weakly. "Then you better find a takeaway that delivers to wagons with no fixed address."

I stick out my tongue at him. Yeah, real classy, I know. And I don't care. Today I'm antisocial, and I'm not going to pretend that I like being around people.

But annoyingly, he's right. The only way to get food is to leave the wagon and in his state, even I can't ask Benjamin to do that. That would amount to torture and as much as I love a bit of torture, I don't like doing it to my employees. It would set a bad precedent.

Grumbling, I leave the wagon and head into town. The weather is great and the streets are full of people. Don't they all have better things to do than getting in my way and rubbing against me? I don't have the patience to go to my favourite butcher's shop today, so instead I enter the first one I pass. Gorgeous, succulent meat awaits me. I have to stop myself from drooling as I take in the food on offer. If that pesky butcher weren't looking at me, I'd climb over the counter and lie down on that mattress of steaks.

"What can I do for ya?" he asks with a friendly smile.

His smile wavers when I start listing everything I want.

"Having a party?" he asks weakly after I've finished my order with two pounds of black pudding. The bloody variant.

"Hungry guests," I retort, giving him a toothy grin.

His eyes widen and he quickly gets started on packing everything up. When he's done, I realise that I'm not going to be able to carry all of that. I'd need a cart to get it all home in one go. My grin widens as I have an idea. I don't need a cart. I have something much better.

I pay and take as many of the bags with me as I can, telling the butcher I'll be back for the rest shortly. In an alley just behind the shop, I set it all down and put two fingers in my mouth, whistling in a pitch too high for humans to hear.

Meow.

A dark ginger cat, so fluffy she almost looks overweight, jumps from a bin at the end of the alleyway and prances towards me.

"Pan," I greet her. "Haven't seen you in a while."

She inclines her head and rubs against my legs. She's one of Ryker's most trusted friends, which is very helpful, considering what I'm about to do. I wait until about a dozen cats have joined us - including Storm, James and tiny Nyx - before crouching on the ground to be closer to their eye level.

"I've got several bags of meat that need to be brought to the wagon we're staying at. I assume you all know where it is?"

Pan nods, her eyes glinting.

"Good. You take one bag each. If I find anything missing, I won't be happy." I glare at them, satisfied when the youngest cats shrink back a little. I haven't lost my touch. "You'll get a share once I'm back, but I warn you, don't take even the smallest bite. Or else. Understood?"

As soon as I sense their assent, I get up and hand out bags of meat. It works out perfectly, I only have one left when they all have one, and Pan takes that one off me. She's big enough to carry two.

They run off, some a little slow because their bags are too big, but I'm sure they'll manage. Cats are ingenious if there's food as a reward. I snicker when I realise that the same applies to me in this very moment. Using cats as carriers. Brilliant. I'll never have to carry my shopping ever again. This is so much cheaper than having it delivered too.

I return to the butcher's and take the rest of the meat. He gives me a strange look but I ignore him. Next time, I'll go to my favourite butcher shop again, where I know the meat is organic and straight from the fields, so to speak. Before I start my walk home, I return to the alley and open one of the bags. Lamb shanks. Perfect. I wolf them down, moaning in contentment as my taste buds go in overdrive. I have to remind myself to chew because the predator in me wants to do nothing but rip and swallow. I'm human just now, though, and I'll end up with a stomach ache if I'm not careful.

The meat is fresh and bloody. I ram my teeth into the flesh and suck out the juice. Not as good as the wolves' blood earlier, but still satisfying. At this moment, I don't even care that this is not normal behaviour, not even for a shifter. All I can focus on is the meat, the blood, the scent of dead prey.

By the time I'm done, blood is smeared all over my face and hands. I clean myself up as best as I can, then start the journey home. I no longer mind being surrounded by humans. On the contrary. It's like I'm in the middle of a free supermarket, full of yummy, blood-filled prey. I'd only have to reach out and rip out someone's throats to-

I stop in my tracks. Someone bumps into me from behind, mutters something nasty, but I'm frozen in place. I just thought about killing *humans*. Not because I assassinate them as my job, but for food. A shiver runs down my back. Something is very, very wrong with me. I've never had that urge before, not even when shifted. Humans and cats are out of bounds. They're not food.

I grab my bags and start running, away from the tempting smells and sounds of the crowd. I need to get to safety before I kill someone.

RYKER AND LENNOX HAVEN'T RETURNED YET, BUT Gryphon is back, sitting outside the wagon, his eyes closed, his legs outstretched. He's enjoying the sun. I wish I could do the same. I run inside and drop the bags of meat. Several others are already on the kitchen floor, watched over by Benjamin.

"I guess this is your doing?" he asks while pouring oil into a frying pan.

"Seemed like a good way to get all that food home." I shrug, forcing myself to appear calm, even though I want to quite literally jump out of my skin.

"What did you promise them in return?"

"A share of the meat, I wasn't very specific."

He throws two steaks into the pan. The sizzling sound almost makes me rip them out of there and eat them raw. Meat isn't supposed to be cooked. Is it? My head is starting to hurt. I need someone to tell me what's going on.

"I've already given Pan some of the meat as a reward," Benjamin says, unaware of the turmoil in my mind. "They've run off; it seemed to be enough. Ryker will be grateful, I think he's been having trouble finding enough food for all his cats, now that more and more have joined his family."

I wasn't aware of that. I should be, though. Ryker's a friend. More than a friend. I should know when he has a problem and I should be there to support him. Fuck. I feel even worse now.

I was going to go outside to talk to Gryphon, but I can't control myself anymore. I'm scared I might fall apart completely if I try and explain what I'm feeling. I run into my bedroom and close the door behind me before dropping onto the mattress, burying my face in my hands. I don't think I've ever felt this weak and afraid.

I curl up into a ball, pressing my face into the sheets. The bed smells of the guys. Ryker, who I disappointed. Lennox, whose wolf bond I refused. Gryphon, who-

The door barges open and he strides in. I lift my head, knowing I should pretend I'm not about to cry, but then the floodgates open and there's no holding back. He's by my side in an instant, taking me into his arms. I fight him; I don't deserve to be comforted, but he holds me tight, pressing me against his chest. If I wanted to, I could easily escape his grip, but the weak, crying Kat who's taken over is craving the closeness. I let him stroke my hair, hating myself for the vulnerability I'm allowing him see. Tears keep streaming from my eyes and I'm unable to stop them. Yet another thing I don't have control over. That thought only makes me cry even more. I've lost control of my life, of everything, and it makes me fucking weak.

"Talk to me, Kat," Gryphon mutters. "I can't help if I don't know what's going on."

I can't. I don't even know myself what the problem is. I no longer feel like myself, but how can I explain that? I'm losing myself, I'm disappearing, and because I don't know what's happening, I can't fight it.

"Kat, tell me," he tries again. "Please."

That last word breaks my heart. He sounds so desperate. Just like I feel.

But there's no way I can open up. If he finds out

that I'm craving blood and human flesh, he's going to turn away from me in disgust. He's going to leave me and will take the others with him. I startle at my own thoughts. When did I become so needy? I shouldn't be scared of him leaving me. I'm a cat, I thrive in my own company. I don't need people around me. I don't need friends. I can go back to it being just me against the world.

"I'm sorry I have to do this," he whispers, and before I realise what he's about to do, he starts to sing. His siren powers fill the room, crawl over my skin, enter my mind. His music is beautiful, out of this world. It hugs me, soothes me, warms me from the inside. I let it in, craving its touch.

It tells me not to struggle and I believe it. The music sinks through all the cracks in my walls, seeping into my broken soul. I close my eyes and let myself drift, dimly feeling Gryphon's embrace, his warmth.

His song turns more intense as it takes hold of me. It whispers to me, but I can't understand the words, not even their intentions. I don't feel threatened, though. On the contrary, I know I'm safe. Really safe for the first time in ages. Nobody can touch me while I'm in Gryphon's arms. He's protecting me from the outside world. I don't need to be strong. I can let go of my pain. Share it. Break it into pieces and give them to the people who care about me.

Slowly, the song changes. The words start to make sense. They're a message and this time, I listen.

"I'm broken," I tell the music. "Something's wrong with me. Ever since I was captured by the Pack, I've been having strange cravings. New feelings. I think I'm changing."

The words tumble from my lips. I talk about it all. The blood lust. The urge to be alone, to push everyone away. The new strength. The way I craved human flesh.

I let it all out, not holding anything back. I know this is a safe space. The music won't judge me. Whenever I say something, she praises me, strokes my skin, soothes the pain. Talking about it doesn't hurt as much as I thought. It actually makes me feel better. The hole in my chest is slowly closing.

"Thank you," the music says. "We'll figure it out. I promise. We'll make you better."

No, not the music. That's Gryphon's voice, surrounded by song. I don't know how he does it, speaking while also making this beautiful music, but I don't care.

I snuggle against him, content knowing that he's not judging me. He said I'm going to get better. I'm not sure I believe him, but in this moment, I don't care. Who knows, he might be right. His music is showing me how powerful he really is.

The song gets fainter until it drifts into the air, echoing in my ears but no longer seeping into my mind. I'm not being held by the music, but by Gryphon's muscular body.

"Thank you," he whispers and presses a tiny kiss on my forehead. "I'm sorry you had to deal with that on your own."

"I'm sorry too."

I open my eyes and sit up, startled by the new voice.

Ryker and Lennox are standing by the door, looking at me with expressions I can't read.

The warm feeling in my belly dissipates. Now they know.

Fuck.

CHAPTER FIVE

"Don't run." Ryker slowly approaches the mattress, his eyes locked with mine. "We need to talk about this."

Gryphon's hold on me tightens. "He's right," he mutters in my ear, while his hands stroke my back. "Let's see if we can't find a way to help you. Together. All of us."

I groan. I'm the centre of attention now, but not in a good way.

Ryker sits on the bed and Lennox joins us on the other side, lying next to me so that his body touches mine. Ryker stretches out an arm and takes my hand. I let him. All three of them are touching me and it feels good. It's not a sexual thing at all. Just closeness that strengthens the bond between us. The bond that I've been rejecting as hard as I could.

I should probably sit up properly and talk to them like a grown-up, but instead, I close my eyes again and snuggle into Gryphon's hug. I'm still working on putting up my walls again. Right now I'm fragile and I need them to know that. If they're not careful, they might break me. *Be gentle with my little soul.* Now I know what that old folk song is all about.

"We didn't hear the beginning, but to summarise, you're becoming more feral," Ryker says after clearing his throat. It's obvious he's trying to keep his voice calm and soothing. I can almost hear him purr. "Like more of your panther is seeping into your human self while also becoming stronger when you're shifted. And it's all got something to do with what happened at the lab."

"Take us through that again." Lennox gently strokes my thigh. Again, I don't think his intentions are sexual, even though he's touching me in a place usually reserved for intimacy. "We know they starved you. Tortured you. I'm sorry to have to make you talk about it but we need every single detail."

I sigh. I'd hoped never to have to think about that again. "It wasn't *real* torture. Just stabs with that electric rod from time to time."

Gryphon chuckles. "I'd say that's torture."

"Not proper. I can do much worse."

"I don't doubt that. What happened on the day you escaped?"

I let myself drift into the memory. Ryker is still holding my hand and I use him as my anchor who tethers me in the present. It's not as bad knowing that I'm not alone this time.

"They took me to a lab. I was strapped in a chair. I couldn't move because of the effects of that rod. The siren came in. He said I'd been there before but that I couldn't remember. Then he showed me photographs. First of Doctor Fitzroy, then of two young men, then the Original. The woman whose clone I am. And then a picture of Mystery Man." I swallow hard. "Professor Lakefield. That's when he told me the truth. I was devastated. But then a switch flicked inside of me and I felt strong."

"A switch?" Gryphon asks. "Can you explain that?"

I laugh. "I wish I could. It's like I broke through a wall that had always been there, and behind it was pure power. I'd fed off the power that had seeped through the wall before, but now I had access to it all. I was able to break my bonds and kill the siren."

"Do you think it's your cat's energy?" Lennox asks. "I feel like that sometimes. When I'm human, I'm separated from my wolf, but I still have access to a fraction of his power. When I shift, this reverses and I'm all wolf and can only use some of my human skills."

I shake my head. "No, it's more than that. It's like it's not just my cat, but *more*. The power of her multiplied, but not just the power, also her instincts and urges."

"Which is why you feel more feral," he says slowly. "And why you crave meat. I doubt it's just human flesh. If we put you in front of a cow, you might want to eat it too."

Saliva pools in my mouth at the thought of beef fresh from the cow. Bloody, juicy, still warm. Hot liquid running down my throat.

"You're right," I say once I've managed to push that

image out of my mind. "I've got the same cravings for cows now. Got one close by?"

Luckily, they ignore that question.

Gryphon runs his hand through my hair. I don't like people touching my hair. Normally. Not today, though. A purr rumbles through my chest.

He chuckles. "I love it when you do that."

I elbow him in the chest and he shuts up.

"Our cat's got her claws out again," Lennox says with a soft laugh. "But back to the issue at hand. We need to find out what happened in that lab."

"I just told you."

"No, I mean in the past. They took you there as a child and did goodness what with you. We found reports of them having a drug they gave to shifters, so maybe it's related to that. Or it might have been experiments we don't know anything about yet. Whatever it was, I bet it's related to your current problems. Being in the same lab again, and being threatened, triggered something."

"Maybe the twins know something," Gryphon suggests. "I think we should do a sister meeting. You, the twins, Little Kat. If you compare notes, you might be able to fill in the gaps."

I sigh. "I need to talk to them anyway. We need to find the rest of us. They mentioned K2 and K7, plus two of us are dead." I don't want to say K3 and K6. I won't use those terms. They deserve a name and until I find out if they had one, I'm not going to call them by their designation. "There are others out there. What if they have the same problems I have, but without people like you to support them?"

I finally open my eyes and sit up, looking at the three guys. "I hate to admit this, but I'd never be able to get through this without you."

Ryker squeezes my hand. "Thank you for saying that. I know how hard it is for you to acknowledge that you can't do everything on your own."

A trickle of anger flows through me, but he's right. I'm used to dealing with every problem myself. I have a team, yes, but they only support me with things I could do myself if I had the time. I just can't be bothered. And yes, Bethany is better with poisons than me and I couldn't do the seducing Lily does, but… alright, I need my team. Not that I'd tell them that. I don't want them to demand a pay rise.

"There's one more thing we need to talk about," Ryker says hesitantly. "Yesterday, you ran away. Why?"

An invisible fist clenches around my heart. The other stuff, the hunger, the bloodlust, that I can explain away, blame it on whatever experiments the Pack did on me. But I'm not sure if me pushing the guys away is part of that or whether that's just the way I am.

"I'm not good with…" I sigh, trying to find the words. "…with letting people close. It's hard enough with one, but there's three of you and you all have expectations that I'm not sure I can fulfil."

"We don't need you to sleep with us," Gryphon says, but I interrupt him.

"That's not the problem. Sex is easy. I'd have no problem fucking you. One, two, all at once. Well, never done the latter but I'm sure it would be fun. The problem is everything that comes with it. You're not random guys I chose to spend a night with, one night only. You're here for something more, something deeper. And I'm worried I'll mess it up."

I can't meet their eyes. It must be the aftereffect of Gryphon's music that makes me talk this open with them. I can't believe I said all that. So embarrassing.

"We're all in this together." Lennox puts his hands on my shoulders to underline his words. "I don't know about the others, but I've never been in a relationship. Like you, I've chosen random people to scratch my urges-"

"Scratch your balls, you mean," Ryker interrupts with a laugh.

"Fuck off. I'm new to this too. I don't have a clue what I'm doing, and I certainly never expected to share you. But that's fine. I want you and if that means I can't be your only one, then that's fine. We can go as fast or as slow as you want. If you need time, that's fine. You just need to talk to us. If you don't want to sleep in a bed with all of us, we'll find an alternative."

"What he said," Gryphon muttered. "We don't want you to be uncomfortable around us."

My eyes are itching again. Fuck those feelings. I don't want to be emotional, but I'm still feeling the aftereffects of the siren's song. I should be angry at him for doing that to me, but I'm not. It feels strangely good to have told them what's going on. I thought it would be embarrassing to admit the changes I'm going through. In fact, I'm now embarrassed that I didn't tell them in the first place.

"Kat." Lennox entwines his fingers with mine, gently rubbing my knuckles. "You already know that my wolf wants you to be his mate. I'm bound to you and I wouldn't change it for the world."

I sneeze. "Sorry. I think I'm allergic to sappiness."

CHAPTER SIX

The twins arrive just when dinner is ready. I'm sure they planned it that way. Bethany has cooked, which means it's pretty good. She knows her way around herbs – perk of being a poisons expert. I still wish my steak was a little rawer, but I'm not going to show that. As much as I like my humans, sharing with the guys has been enough for today. I'm not going to involve Lily, Beth and Benjamin in my problems. They can be part of our search for my sisters and our fight against the Pack – what's left of it, anyway – but that's it. My personal issues are mine to deal with.

"Now I know why you keep them around," Ivy says while chewing loudly. Their table manners suck just as much as my own. Gryphon looks a little piqued at how we're not using cutlery in the correct way, but he's the only posh one in the group. Lennox grew up in the Pack, Benjamin on the streets, no idea about Bethany, Lily's family didn't much care about manners and Ryker hasn't been human for very long. In short, there's a lot of gnawing, loud munching, and screeching knives.

"We've not eaten at a table for a while," Four admits. "This is kind of nice."

I have so many questions about how they grew up and what they've been through, but now isn't the time. I'm still rebuilding my walls. I'd probably start crying if I heard their sob story now.

When we're done, Bethany dishes up dessert. Warm chocolate pudding with cream. All four felines in the room moan in contentment when the cream is passed around.

Beth laughs. "I was hoping you'd all have Kat's usual reaction to cream. Totally makes it worth buying this quantity."

"Did you get catnip too?" I ask, hopeful. "That would be quite a spectacle."

"No catnip," Lily says with a stern frown. "Not after last time. I'm not letting you turn into an addict."

I shrug. "I can control it."

"No. You can't. Or do you want me to tell them about the string incident?"

I glare at her. "Don't you dare, or I'll fire you."

"As if. You love me far too much."

I sigh. "Yeah. I do. Now pass me some more of that cream or I'll get cranky."

She grins and a warmth spreads in my belly that has nothing to do with chocolate pudding. This is how it used to be. Joking around, not a care in the world. I'm glad we can still have these moments, even though they've become rare. Once we've solved all our problems, I'm going to lock us all into our new house and force everyone to play board games and do other mundane stuff. Maybe with a bit of dissection fun in the morgue. Oh yes, the new house needs a morgue, and a lab, and a better cooling chamber than our old headquarters. That one always broke and made our corpses mouldy.

Soon. A few more weeks of hard work and then I can find us a new home.

When we're done, I let Lily do the dishes while Benjamin disappears back to bed. He still looks pretty ill so it's probably good for him to stay away from the other humans. They catch diseases so easily. And yes, I'm counting Lily as human in this case. She's half-succubus, but her immune system is ridiculously bad.

I turn to the twins. "Let's make plans. You said there's another Pack lab that hasn't been destroyed?"

Four nods. "Yes, that's the one guarded by K2."

"What?"

They exchange a look. "We never got to tell you last time. I think we got distracted with what M.E.O.W. stands for. Which you still haven't told us, by the way."

"K2 is completely controlled by them," Ivy explains. "She's exactly how they hoped we'd all turn out. Pliable, listens to every command and very, very strong. Also completely psychotic. Sometimes I wonder if they took away all her humanity somehow."

"There must be a way to get her out and fix her," I start, but they both shake their heads.

"We tried," Four says with a sigh. "Several times. We managed to sneak into her room once to talk to her. She attacked right away, didn't listen at all. She also didn't seem to be surprised to hear that she's a clone. They must have told her, not like with you and us. And the third time we confronted her, she captured Ivy. I barely managed to break her out."

Ivy grimaces. "It wasn't a ruse either. She hurt me, bad. Took me forever to recover from that. But while she was torturing me, I looked into her eyes and they were empty. She isn't like us. She doesn't have a soul."

I highly doubt that, but I don't say anything. I'll have to see it for myself. I don't want to give up on one of my sisters. She may be completely brainwashed, but there might be a way back. Gryphon's siren power could help, who knows.

If not… I don't think I could kill her.

"Does she have a name?" I ask the twins. "Besides K2?"

Four shrugs. "I doubt it. She's not independent enough to think that she might want one. You'll know when you see her. She's brainwashed or maybe she's always been that way. She believes the Pack are worth protecting and that we are the enemies. She won't hesitate to kill us if she gets the chance."

"And she guards the lab? Permanently?" Gryphon asks.

"She's been there every time we tried to get in," Ivy replies. "So unless it's one massive coincidence, we're pretty sure it's her task to protect the lab. It's the place we know the least about. If we've been in there before, then it's been part of the erased memories. That's why we need to get inside and find out what they're hiding.

We feel like there's an important piece of the puzzle hidden in that lab."

I notice once again how the twins keep talking about themselves as 'we'. I wonder what it would be like to have a sister. Someone who's completely identical. No, I wouldn't wish that on anyone. One Kat is enough for this world. Two of us would probably end up as archenemies.

Then I remember that there are at least ten of me. Not quite the same, as I've realised now that I've met both Little Kat and the twins, but still, we're more similar than normal sisters would be. We've been raised in different ways, but our genes are the same, unless the Pack have messed with that.

Let's hope we won't turn into enemies.

ASSASSINS WORK BEST IN THE DARK OF NIGHT. SO DO cats. We've decided not to wait and delay any further. Ryker has rallied some of his cats while the rest of us are getting ready. I'm back in my leather assassin outfit. How I missed wearing this. The leather hugs me like a second skin, while still being thick enough to hide weapons and ward off weak attacks. My boots steady me both physically and mentally. I could kiss my team for saving some of my clothes when our house went up in flames. It seems the fires were set on the ground floor, so it took a while for the flames to reach the attic where I used to live.

Gryphon and Lennox are clad in black as well,

blending into the night. The moon is hidden beneath thick clouds, giving us even better cover. The M.E.O.W. team is staying at home. Usually, I'd take Benjamin with me since he's the best at breaking and entering, but he's too sick. He'd end up being a liability in his current state.

The twins have raided Lily's closet (which is surprisingly well-stocked, even after the fire), not because they needed new clothes, but because they were bored. Ivy now wears a skirt that is way too short for someone her age, and Four is spouting a frilly top that's supposed to be filled with cleavage she doesn't yet have. They look ridiculous, but I leave them be. As long as Ivy can run and fight in that skirt, I'm okay with it. It's not like I'm their mum.

"You can fight, right?" I ask them out of the blue.

Four looks at me as if I'm crazy. "How do you think we survived this long?"

"Four was raised by the Pack," Ivy explains. "Not here, at a facility in the countryside. And before you ask, it no longer exists. We made sure of that. I wasn't taught any fighting skills by my carers but Four taught me via our connection."

"Connection?" I ask.

"Long story." Four turns away as if we're talking about the most boring topic ever. "We can hear each other's thoughts."

"More like *feel* each other's minds," Ivy corrects. "I always know what she's feeling. It's like my own emotions. It took us years to separate them. I kept crying without knowing why until I realised it was Four who was sad. I think we always knew that the other existed, even as toddlers, but we didn't see each other until we were what, nine?"

"Ten." Four isn't looking at us. "And then they tried to separate us again, two years ago. Big mistake."

Wow. My mind is reeling. I kind of want to hug them, which is so out of character for me that I stop to think before I say anything else. Let's not get sentimental. They might not respect me if I start acting all emotional.

A cat rubs against my legs. Storm, black as the night, but her azure eyes give her away. I reach down to rub her head. She purrs before walking over to Ryker. I envy the way he can talk to them even though he's human just now. I can only read their intentions, and they can understand me, but if I want to have a proper conversation with a cat, I need to shift. I guess living among them all his life has given Ryker this advantage.

"They're ready," he announces and everyone turns to him. "I've got cats surrounding the building as we speak. By the time we get there, they'll be able to give us a full report."

I straighten my back and crack my knuckles. "Good, then let's head out. We've got answers to find and a lab to destroy."

CHAPTER SEVEN

Four and Ivy seem just as at home on the roofs as me. They're lighter and slightly smaller, but my new strength makes me faster than everyone else. I try not to draw on it too much. I don't want to start craving blood again. Right now, I feel normal, but who knows how long that will last. Although I don't really care if I kill everyone inside the lab. That's a place I'm allowed to break into a frenzy. I both hope and dread that we'll find answers there. While we're running across town, I prepare mentally for what may await us. I can deal with guards and Pack members. K2 is the unknown variable this time. I don't want to believe the twins about her, but I need to be ready just in case she really is brainwashed, conditioned to fight her own sisters. If she attacks us, attacks my guys or the twins, then I'll have to act. I won't be the first to draw the sword, but I will defend us with all the strength I possess. The plan is to take her alive though, and then raid the lab.

I very rarely venture into this part of town. There's

not much here besides simple dwellings. Not poor enough to house the seedy individuals I sometimes do business with, and not rich enough to rob. Not important enough to assassinate. There's no reason I have to go here, which is why it's a perfect hiding place for a Pack lab. No one would ever suspect something like that here, among the boring semi-detached brick houses and dirty streets. As far as I know, there's not even a shop in this area. Dull.

We don't speak until we reach a roof not far from the lab. I can smell Ryker's cats from here. The twins have described to him where the lab is so that he could send his friends up ahead. I think Four and Ivy are a little jealous of my feline surveillance network. I reach down and pet Storm again. They should be jealous. My cats are amazing.

It surprises me a little that the lab is still going. I can see the lights from here; people are working even at this hour. Killing the Pack's leaders hasn't stopped them. Maybe they've been working on their own agenda for a while, or maybe they're being controlled by forces higher up than the Pack. Not much longer and we'll hopefully have answers.

An older cat with grey whiskers runs up to Ryker and meows his report.

"They can sense at least five humans inside, plus other beings they can't identify. Not sirens, they know Gryphon's scent too well to get that confused."

"Those mutant grunts maybe?" I suggest.

"Could well be. They haven't found a scent that resembles yours, but the building is several storeys high and none of the cats has gone inside, so K2 could be in there without us knowing. If she's not left the lab in a few days, there wouldn't be a good scent of her outside. Cat senses only go so far."

Storm hisses and I give her a soothing head rub. "Your senses are way better than dogs'," I tell her earnestly and she snuggles against my leg. I like Storm; I think I should spend more time with her. When I'm shifted, she looks like she could be my baby with her silky black coat, even though she's older than me.

"Is everyone ready?" I ask and look around my team. The guys give me sharp nods, all business, while the twins look impatient to get going. The cats… well, they're being cats, begging for head rubs and attention.

"You all know what to do. Let's burn this place to the ground."

I take a deep breath, steadying myself. Immediately, my senses intensify. The world becomes sharper and brighter as I push some of my shifter energy to my eyes. My night vision is excellent even when human, but now I see as much as if it were broad daylight. My hearing increases so much that I can hear the heartbeat of the human sleeping in the house below us. She doesn't know she's got several assassins on her roof.

One last check to see that my knives are where they should be, then I'm off, jumping onto the roof opposite, now in full view of the lab. It's a tall building that really doesn't belong in this part of town. Tall, sleek, lots of glass. I'm looking forward to breaking it. I bet it would look great if all the glass were to shatter at the same time, raining down like sharp bits of snow. I grin at the thought. There's always something to look forward to.

I crouch low, just in case guards are down there. I bet there are, even if nobody can be seen from the outside. Gryphon said they're using the same siren technology we've encountered before, the high-pitched sounds that make people turn away without knowing why. Luckily, that doesn't work on any of us. Another reason why it was good to have the humans stay home.

I stay on the roof while I wait for the others to get into position. Storm lands next to me like a shadow in the night. Which she is, more or less. A fluffy shadow who wants to be petted.

"Are you sure you're a cat and not a lovesick little dog?" I whisper. She hisses but still keeps pressing her head against my hand, demanding cuddles. She's totally taking advantage of me having to wait for the others. Devious.

I pet her absentmindedly while watching the entrance of the lab. Tall blinds hide the interior, but thanks to Ryker's cats we already know how many people are inside, at least how many there are on the ground floor. I could have probably found out myself by sitting out here for a while and letting my shifter senses free reign, but that would require me to be patient, and tonight I'm anything but. This lab might hold the answers I crave. The faster I get in, the better.

It seems to take forever for Gryphon to arrive at the lab's front doors. If there's any siren security tech, he should be able to get through and disable it for the rest of us. It's very convenient to have a siren on our side, especially one so gorgeous as him. I can't help but ogle his arse as he slowly walks into the building. His black jeans are particularly tight today. He should wear those more often.

Storm meows approvingly.

"He's a bit big for you," I whisper. "Besides, he's mine."

It feels good saying that. Mine. The cat in me purrs. Talking about it all really did help. It'll still take some time for me to get used to the idea of actually being in a relationship, but for now, I'm happy to claim them as mine.

The light inside the lab flickers. That's the signal. Gryphon's dispatched whatever guards were waiting for us in the reception area. Two shadows approach the doors. Ryker and Lennox. They sneak in, joining Gryphon. I'm a little jealous they get to have all the fun, while I'm out here, watching from afar. Screams echo from the building, too quiet for any humans to hear. I grimace. So unfair. I want to play too. Hopefully, they'll leave some for me. Although that would defeat the reason why I'm not going in knives blazing. This is all to prevent me from going into another blood frenzy. I need to keep my cool if I want to find the information I need and confront K2. The twins don't know that; they think I'm out here to coordinate everything.

I wait while stroking Storm's silky fur. She's really taking full advantage of the situation. Well, I would have done the same thing. We're alike in that way.

Finally, the lights flash again. It's showtime. I climb off the roof, easily finding footholds in the brick wall. I love old buildings like that, they're so much easier to scale. The glass lab would have been so much harder to climb, which is why we're going through the front doors. We're strong enough to give up the advantage of stealth and make a full-blown frontal attack. I just hope we're not too cocky. There's a reason this lab is still going even though the Pack leaders are dead.

The twins appear out of nowhere, taking their places at my side as we stroll into the building, followed by several cats. The smell of death permeates my senses. Three bodies lie on the floor, blood pooling around them. Hunger blooms inside of me, but I push it down. I can't afford to lose control now, no matter how tasty they look.

"I can sense her," Four suddenly says, freezing in mid-step. "She's here."

"K2?" I ask, pulling my knives from their sheaths.

She nods. "She's close. Stay on guard."

The guys wait for us near a staircase with steps leading both up and down.

"Any idea where she could be?" Ivy asks her sister.

Four turns in a circle, her eyes closed. "Upstairs. I think. It's hard to tell. There are some of those mutants too."

I groan. "I was dreading that. They're such a bother to kill."

I turn to the guys. "Lennox, Ryker, you take the basement. Gryphon, you're with us. If K2 gives us trouble, you might be able to use some of your siren tricks on her. Remember, we want to take her alive. No killing my sister."

Ivy scoffs. "She's not our sister. She's too far gone."

I glare at her. "We're not giving up on one of our own. No killing."

She mutters something under her breath, but I try not to listen. I don't want any division between us just now; we need to focus.

I run up the stairs, hoping that everyone else will follow.

"Wait!" Ryker calls out. "I'm sending some of the cats with you. They can carry messages if need be."

Of course, Storm decides to come with me, together with two other female cats that I don't know yet. The larger one is a tabby with a furry golden belly, the other is tiny and looks completely bored, as if she doesn't give a flying fuck over the current situation.

The rest of them follow Ryker into the basement. It's hard to imagine doing anything nowadays without being surrounded by a bunch of moggies. They do come in handy and I guess they're a good distraction too.

"She's close," Four whispers from behind me.

I sniff the air while taking two steps at a time. I can't make out anything but human scents mixed with a bit of siren. Whatever Four is doing to sense K2, I can't do it. Once we're done with this, I'm going to have to find out what other skills the twins possess. Maybe we can teach each other stuff, or at least take advantage of the others' abilities.

The staircase isn't ending. It seems to skip the first floor and leads us straight to the second one. Weird. A glass door separates a corridor from the stairwell. I'm tempted to send Gryphon to the next floor, but we might need him. It seems a little overkill to take three other people with me, but if the twins are right about how strong K2 is, it might be necessary.

Our footsteps echo through the empty corridor, even though all four of us are experts in walking quietly. We take turns checking the doors on either side, but all of them are boring offices, most containing nothing but a desk, chair and some shelves. I hope we'll find the information we need somewhere else and don't have to go through each of these rooms. That would be the dullest task ever.

"She's-"

Before Four can complete her sentence, a blur of movement makes me look up just in time to see someone drop from the ceiling. From the fucking ceiling, like a spider. She lands in a crouch in front of us, blocking the way. Usually, I'd use my knives to attack right away, but I recognise her from the way she moves. She's me. My sister. She's my size, but a little thinner, and her hair is cut short. She's all in white, a stark contrast from the black the rest of us are clad in. She doesn't say anything. She just attacks.

She jumps, flying through the air, right at me. I let myself drop on all fours, just about managing to evade her, but Gryphon isn't so lucky. She hits him in the chest and both of them go down. He cries out and I'm hit by the smell of blood. Fuck. I jump to my feet and attack her from behind, trying to pull her off him. The twins join me, each of them grabbing one of her arms. Her fingers drip with Gryphon's blood. Claws sit where her fingernails should be. She doesn't seem to have any weapons, but she's moved way faster than I ever could, so it's no surprise she doesn't need any.

She fights against our grip, but there's three of us and all of us are strong, even the twins, despite being smaller than me.

"Gryphon, are you alright?" I shout while wrapping my legs around hers, trying to keep her in check.

"I'm fine." He stumbles to his feet, exposing deep gashes on his chest. He's bleeding a lot, but there's nothing I can do about that for now.

Suddenly, K2 starts to shake, as if she's having a fit. I hold onto her, even though she seems to be getting heavier.

"Look at her hands!" Ivy shouts.

Wow. Her claws are lengthening, growing until they're almost as long as her lower arm. What. The. Meowing. Fuck. This isn't a partial shift, it's something far more than that. What have they done to her?

She kicks me and pain shoots through my shins, but I manage to keep a hold on her. The smell of my own blood fills the corridor, mixing with that of Gryphon. I can't see it from here, but she must have the same claws on her feet. It hurts like hell. It only seems to be a flesh wound though; at least I can move my legs as normal, so no sinews or bones seem to be injured.

"Gryphon, your voice!" I shout, knowing we won't be able to hold on to her for much longer. The twins are having a hard time trying to evade her claws as they clutch K2's arms.

Black fur starts to sprout on her neck. Oh no, you don't. Without thinking, I sink my teeth into her neck, biting down as hard as I can. She squeals, the first sound she's made ever since she started attacking us. Her blood pours into my mouth. It tastes sour, like milk that's been out of the fridge for too long. Definitely not the way blood should taste, shifter or not. Whatever the Pack scientists have done to her, it's changed her way more than the twins or me. Maybe they were right about her being too far gone to be saved.

Gryphon opens his mouth and music touches my skin, embracing me like an old friend. I smile, but I don't let it relax me too much. We're still fighting. The fur slowly starts to recede and pale skin retakes its place. I don't understand the words of the siren's song, but they're not meant for me anyway. He's singing for K2, soothing her. She's no longer struggling as much and her claws slowly start to shrink. I didn't think it would be this easy to tame her, so it comes as a bit of a surprise. I still keep my teeth in her neck though and my grip on her tight. She might just be pretending.

Gryphon is taking his time, slowly wrapping her into his music. It makes me all warm and fuzzy. And a bit jealous that he's singing for K2, who attacked him and really doesn't deserve it. When we're home, I might ask him to sing for me again.

"Yes," she whispers.

I exchange a look with the twins. Why did she say that?

"Yes," she repeats. "I promise."

It must have something to do with the music. Gryphon smiles at her, although the pain is evident on his face by now. His skin is turning pale, making his scars look way more pronounced than usual. Slowly, he ends his song, letting the music trail off in a way that makes the echo chime in my head for several breaths. Beautiful.

"You can let go of her now," he says just before he collapses.

I drop K2 and run to Gryphon, kneeling by his side.

"Sorry," he mutters.

"What the fuck are you apologising for?"

I inspect his wounds. They're deeper than I first thought and are bleeding a lot. I'm going to kill K2 for hurting my man. No, I won't, but I might torture her a little. Nobody hurts my siren.

"I can help." Ivy kneels by my side. "But I'll have to lick him."

I gape at her. "Lick him?"

"My saliva contains healing enzymes. Four's too, but mine's stronger. It won't be enough to fully heal his wounds, but it should stop the blood flow."

"You want to lick Gryphon," I repeat slowly. "I think that's the weirdest thing I've ever said."

She laughs softly. "Trust me, I'm not usually into licking men. I've only ever done this to one other person besides my sister. Voluntarily, that is." Her expression darkens. "Of course the Pack took full advantage of that ability."

My stomach clenches at the thought of what my sisters have been forced to do. They're still young, children almost, yet they've been through more than anyone ever should have to. How I hate the Pack. I'm looking forward to torching this building and killing anyone still inside.

"Do it," Gryphon bites out between clenched teeth.

I look away when she bends down to lick his chest. That's just weird.

He sighs and I frown at him. It almost sounds like he enjoys it.

His relieved smile instantly vanishes from his face.

"So unpleasant," he groans theatrically.

Four clears her throat. "When you're done licking each other, could we deal with K2?"

I get up and approach my two sisters. Four is holding a knife to K2's throat, but the older girl isn't reacting to it at all. Her eyes are fixed on Gryphon, but she seems slightly vacant at the same time.

"Do you know who I am?" I ask her. She doesn't take notice of me at all. Her gaze doesn't shift, even though I'm now in between her and Gryphon.

Four looks just as confused as I feel.

"Has she ever been like this when you met her before?"

She shakes her head. "Nope. She's always attacked us, never stopped even for a second. We tried talking to her, but she didn't care. This is completely new."

"I think they must have conditioned her to be very susceptible to a siren's song," Gryphon says from behind me, slowly getting to his feet. "They needed a way to control her, especially since she's not wearing a collar. I bet she only takes instructions from other sirens and follows them until she gets new ones."

That would explain it. And it makes it easier for us

to deal with her. Of course, we won't be able to have Gryphon tell her what to do forever, but it will do for now. Saves us from having to fight her. The twins were right, she really is a much bigger threat than I'd anticipated.

"Can we trust her to not get in the way? Not attack us again?"

Gryphon studies K2 intently. "I'm not sure. I think so, but this is new territory for me too. Nobody ever reacts to my song this quickly. It was like I didn't have to put any effort into it. She just accepted what I was telling her without fighting it. It's creepy, actually. I feel way too powerful and that makes me uncomfortable."

"Most people would be happy to feel powerful," Ivy points out.

"Not Gryphon," I say proudly. "He's different."

He chuckles. "That I am. Shall we proceed? We may have K2 under control, but I bet more obstacles are waiting for us."

"I think you should stay here with her. Lock yourselves into one of the offices while the twins and I explore the rest of the building. You're still wounded and we don't want anyone to take away your control of K2. By the way, can you ask her if she has a name?"

He repeats my question to her.

"K2," she says tonelessly.

Well, that's that then. No name. By now, I doubted it anyway. She doesn't seem to have any personality left.

"I'd rather come with you," Gryphon starts, but I interrupt him.

"Don't protest, you know I'm right. Storm will stay with you. If you need us, send her."

The cats have stayed in the background during the fight, but now that they've heard me mention Storm's name, they approach. The black cat rubs against my legs and I can't resist bending down to give her a quick tickle between the ears.

I wait until the three of them are in one of the offices and have the door locked behind them before I continue walking along the corridor, flanked by the twins. This time, we keep an eye on the ceiling, just in case there's another assassin using it to approach us.

Suddenly, a siren blares to life, blaring through the entire building, making my ears ring. Damn. I'd hoped we'd be able to keep the lab staff from calling for help, but now that it's done, we don't have a choice but prepare for Pack fighters to come. We need to be quick.

The twins keep checking the empty offices while I jog ahead until I reach a set of frosted double doors at the end of the hallway. I stand still and extend my senses. Two people inside, both human. I grip my knives. Finally, I'm going to have some fun.

CHAPTER EIGHT

I throw one knife at the human at the back, a heavy-set man who's hiding behind a table. Stupid of him to peek out right when I barged into the room. The blade embeds itself in his throat and he gurgles as blood spurts from the wound. Delightful.

I launch myself at the other human, a female wearing a guard uniform. She wields two curved daggers and from the way she stands, she knows what she's doing. She grins as she meets my blows as if she's glad to be challenged. I'd be desperate for a fight too if I had to sit in a boring lab all day.

I easily manage to block her strikes, but I have to admit, for a human, she's pretty good. She's definitely not a mutant though; she's too slow for that. I stop myself from going to the offensive, instead deciding to draw out our fight, enjoying every second of it. This is why I do this job. The deep rush of adrenaline. The flashes of clarity. The way the world turns crystal sharp as I anticipate her every move and react to it. I could do this all day.

Something whizzes past my ear and embeds itself in the woman's throat. A knife.

"Hey, I was having fun here," I complain to the twins, then sheathe my weapons.

Four walks over and pulls the blade from the woman's flesh. "We don't have time for fun."

She's right, but this was supposed to be my kill. It leaves a bitter taste in my mouth. Four wipes her knife on her white trousers, leaving bright red bloodstains. Why did the two girls insist on wearing white? It's so impractical on a night like this. There has to be a reason for it, but that story will have to wait for another day.

The lab isn't very big and looks almost exactly like the one where I confronted Grandma Doctor. My neck itches at the thought. She put a collar on me back then and almost killed me. That's not going to happen this time. Fitzroy is dead, so is my other creator. Gryphon and I murdered the Pack leaders. I killed a lot of Pack scientists at the blue house. We're exterminating them one by one like the rats that they are. Hopefully, this is their last lair we need to torch.

Ivy and Four start going through the shelves lining the walls of the lab. I leave them to it and instead take a closer look at the four long tables. They're wiped clean, but there is a scent to my right that seems familiar. I jump over one of the tables - walking around it seems lame - and follow the scent. A narrow drawer is half-open beneath the metal surface, revealing a dozen small flasks. I take one of them and give it a sniff. Yes, that's what I've been smelling.

It reminds me of something but I can't quite put my finger on what that is. Citrus mixed with something sharp that scratches at the back of my throat. I close my eyes and focus on the scent. Another lab...but not a Pack one. My own. Mixed with a different scent, one I smell every day. Bethany. And rubber, the smell of a protective suit.

I open my eyes again, now completely sure where I've come across this before. Bethany was trying to replicate a drug she'd found mentioned in Pack documents. She said it was given to all the clones, but didn't know what it was for. I never found out if she actually managed to successfully produce the substance, but the amber liquid in this little flask must be it.

I'm tempted to drop it and destroy them all, but this might be a part of the puzzle. No, I'm sure it is.

I pocket several of the flasks, then whistle, getting the twins' attention. "Ever seen or smelled this before?"

They come closer, covered in dust from looking through old folders. Yeah, those white clothes have to go.

Ivy gives it a sniff and shakes her head, but Four freezes, her eyes growing wide.

"Where did you find that?"

I point at the desk behind me. "A drawer. I recognised the scent. And so do you, don't you?"

She nods slowly. "Unfortunately."

"Did they give it to you?"

"I think so. It's all a bit blurry."

"At least you remember," Ivy says darkly. "I wish I could."

"You really don't," Four whispers and Ivy grows pale as they exchange a look. Did they just do their mind talk thing?

"Tell me, Four," I say as gently as I can. "What does it do?"

She shakes her head. "I don't want to talk about it."

"I need to know." I almost crush the little flask as I try to stay patient. Her pain is evident. If I were anyone but myself, I'd give her a hug.

Ivy takes her sister's hand. "Shall I tell her?"

Four gives her a grateful smile and nods.

"She's shown me what she can remember," Ivy explains. "And sometimes it's easier for us to let the other do the talking. It's hard to see the memory, but it was a lot harder to live through it."

Yes, I could understand that. I envied them for their unique connection, although I bet it also gave them a lot of pain and torture from the Pack.

"They took her to a lab and strapped her on a chair," Ivy said tonelessly, as if she was reading out a boring document and not recounting her sister's memory. "Then they injected her with this drug. She struggled against the bonds, but she got tired quickly. Then the pain started. Not on her body, in her mind. Her cat was torn from her. The connection between them frayed under the onslaught."

"Wait, what do you mean by that?" I interrupt. "The connection to her cat?"

"They changed us," Four whispers, not meeting my eyes. "They broke us and we can't remember."

"No, we made you better." I have my knives drawn and ready before I realise that the voice came from a speaker above the door. It's a man's voice, deep and threatening.

"I know him," Four mutters beneath her breath.

Instinctively, we've assembled in a triangle, facing out, our backs towards each other.

"Who are you?" I shout.

"Little K1, you're all grown up, and yet you still don't know how to behave. Don't worry, you're going to learn that soon enough."

Who the fuck does he think he is?

"How about you come show yourself and we can talk about this face to face?"

He laughs. "No, I'd rather not. I don't know how you've managed to disable K2, but I'm not taking any chances. I'm having my bears bring you to me instead. Try not to kill too many of them. They're so expensive to produce."

"Did he just say 'bears'?" Ivy asks loudly. "Is he talking about bear shifters? I'm pretty sure they don't exist."

"I hope they don't," I mutter. "If they do, we might be in trouble. Bears are big."

Footsteps approach the lab. I detach five poison darts from my collar and take them between my fingers, ready to throw. They're not as effective on shifters as they are on humans, but they will slow them down, maybe even make them drowsy.

The girls flank me, their own daggers at the ready. I love how we all fight with the same weapons. Maybe it's genetics, maybe it's the way we were trained, who knows, but it makes me feel closer to them.

Before the doors even open, I can smell them.

"They're not bears, they're mutants," I say just as they barge into the room. Six of them. Big, broad brutes wielding swords and axes almost as tall as I am. They're the same grunts I've fought before. The ones whose blood I like to drink.

I grin at the one running towards me. "Hello, darling. I'm going to enjoy sucking you dry." And then I let the darts fly. They're an improved formula, not the ones I had with me when I first attacked one of their kind. Those didn't have any effect. I hope these will. Bethany can usually be trusted with making excellent poisons.

Two of them hit the man at the front, and I've sent one each to three of the other brutes. It's an experiment; let's see if one is enough to bring them down.

Annoyingly, the man now lifting his sword and bringing it down towards me isn't affected by them at all. Shit. I was so sure they'd work. I arch back, crossing my knives in front of my chest to catch his blow. My arms shake as the sword meets my blades. He's fucking strong. Instead of deflecting and then retaliating as I'd planned, I let myself drop to the floor without warning. He stumbles, his balance lost. That's enough time for me to prick him in the ankle with two more darts before rolling out of his reach. Now he finally wavers a little, his eyes turning glassy. He's still not collapsed on the floor like he should be though. I'm going to fire Bethany for this. Or at least halve her salary. She promised me a poison that would be potent enough to work on mutants. Maybe these are different ones, stronger ones. They smell the same, but they do seem a little bigger.

He runs at me again, stumbling, just about managing to catch himself, but now I have two others approaching me. They seem to be brothers, with wild beards and even wilder eyes. Their axes look a little too sharp for my liking. Time to change my strategy.

I take a deep breath and draw on my shifter power. Before, this would have given me some extra strength and the ability to semi-shift, but now, pure energy fills me. When it reaches my mind, it kicks me with the force of half a dozen cocktails. I might have a hangover after this.

I grin and launch myself into battle. When one of the bear-mutants touches my knives with his axe, I push back, surprising both him and me. I twist my hands and with it, his blade, giving me an opening to strike from the side. Annoyingly, his brother isn't waiting for us to finish our fight.

I see his axe coming down towards me from the corner of my eyes and I arch back until my head is almost touching the floor. While the axe cuts the air above me, a hair's breadth from my navel, I flip my knives and stab them into the man's ankles. He screams, and while I know he's going to heal far too soon, it makes him drop to his knees. The perfect height to cut his throat. I do it with my left hand while I stab at the brother with my right. That guy just doesn't get the message.

While one brother squeals - the one with the knife inside his cheek - I squeeze my blade deep into the other's throat. My new strength makes it easy to push through flesh and bone. I let go of the other knife for a second and focus on cutting off the bear's head. He'll heal otherwise and I really don't want to fight him again and again. When his head falls to the floor with a plonk, I kick it to the other side of the room. So satisfying.

The brother roars in anger and rips my blade from his face, leaving a deep gash that exposes the bone beneath. It's barely bleeding though. Those healing abilities really are amazing. I wish I had them.

He picks up his brother's axe, now wielding two of them. Fun. Now that's a real challenge.

The speakers send a second of static before the man's voice fills the room. "Hurry up, I don't have all day."

That's all the distraction I need. While the mutant bear-man listens to his master's words, I dive at him and stab my knife into his chest, twisting as it sinks in. I feel the moment when I reach his heart and his life expires. With the blade inside his heart, even he can't heal quick enough.

He collapses to the floor. I leave that knife in his chest and pick up the other one that he plucked from his cheek. I wipe it on my trousers, glad I'm not wearing white like the twins.

Around me, the sounds of blade meeting blade creates a rhythm, like a drumbeat that my body wants to dance to. Neither of the twins has shouted for help, so I'm assuming they can handle themselves. I need to get rid of my two bears fast though so that I can assist them, just in case. They may be miniature mes, but they're also smaller. Who knows how much fighting experience they really have.

I pull a knife from my boot and turn towards the fight. It's time to dance.

CHAPTER NINE

Four has a great form, but she lacks strength. She's fast though and able to keep out of reach of her opponents' blades while still being able to get in an occasional attack. Ivy is having a more difficult time. She could probably deal with one of the grunts, but right now, two of them are driving her into a corner of the room.

Not happening. I jump onto one of the tables and run along it before launching myself at one of the men. I land on his back, my daggers cutting into the fleshy part where his neck meets his shoulders. He screams like an animal and tries to shake me off. I'm tempted to whoop in delight as he buckles under me like a bull. I've always wanted to try bull riding. I saw that at a travelling fair a couple of years ago but didn't have the money to pay the fee. Now I have my own personal bull. I think I'm going to call him Felix.

I could easily finish him from here, but I'm enjoying

the ride way too much. I let go of him with one hand, just like I'd seen the bull riders do it. That also gives me the chance to throw some poison darts at the man Ivy is fighting. That should make it a little easier for her. Not that I want to mollycoddle my sister, but I don't want her to get hurt either.

Felix is trying to grab me and pull me off his back, but a quick twist of the knives make his arms hang limply by his sides. He roars and this time, I can't help let out a happy cheer. Felix is a great bull. Maybe I should take him home and tame him. The girls could get their own and we could have little competitions.

"Kat, a little help over here!"

Four sounds as if she's in trouble. Urgh. I was having so much fun.

"Shall I kill you or do you want to be my bull?" I ask Felix.

"Kill me," he groans. How boring. I cut his throat, jump off his back and then sever his head from his body. Such a pity. He would have made a great pet.

Four is still fighting two of the grunts and she's no longer making it look as easy as she did before. Multiple thin gashes line her arms where she's not managed to completely evade them, but luckily, the wounds aren't deep. Probably shallow enough for her sister to lick them.

Just when I reach her, she slashes one of the brutes' neck and a fountain of blood rises into the air. Droplets land on my face and without thinking, I lick them from my lips. Sweet nectar fills my mouth. Oh yes. Beautiful.

I no longer care about the fight. All I can think of is my hunger; the craving for the man's blood is overpowering me. From one second to the next, he's on the floor and I'm on top of him, my mouth latched onto this wound. I drink in the blood, swallowing gulps full of the sweet liquid. I've never tasted anything this good. He tries to fight me off but I'm way too strong for him. The world around me turns insignificant. I close my eyes and savour the taste. His blood is like catnip mixed with fresh cream, filling me with happiness. I curl up on top of his now lifeless body and drink my fill. When my thirst is mostly sated, I still don't stop, I just take it slower, lapping up his blood, not wanting to waste a single drop.

A purr rumbles from my chest. I've not been this happy in...forever? This is so much better than catnip. I extend and retract my claws - oh, I have claws now - while running my tongue over his wound to make sure it doesn't close. He's not quite dead yet, I can still hear his slow, weak heartbeat, but the loss of blood has made him unconscious. If I'm lucky, his healing powers will replenish his blood fast enough before he dies. He could be my never-ending fountain of food. I'd never have to buy food again. Free, nutritious, delicious sustenance.

I purr again. I'm living the dream.

"Kat, snap out of it."

There's always one party pooper. I ignore him and take another sip of blood. It makes me feel all warm and fuzzy.

"She's totally stoned. Any idea what to do?"

"Get Gryphon, he'll know."

I let them talk, not caring in the slightest what their

conversation is about. I'm all about the blood. Liquid catnip is the best invention ever.

"Kat?"

It's kind of Gryphon to join me.

"Want some blood?" I slur.

"No. We don't have time for this, there's more coming."

"More blood?"

He groans for some reason. "No, more people wanting to kill us. Can you fight?"

"No way," someone else says. "She's way too out of it. She's a liability."

I raise my head to glare at whoever said that. I'm not a-

My ears flick up as a new sound registers. Footsteps in the distance. Heavy breathing. Fast heartbeats. I count them, even though that's hard.

"Twenty," I mutter, realising that this might be important. Even more important than the yummy blood source I'm lying on.

"Fuck. You, little cat, go and tell Ryker that we need him. I'm not sure if I can keep K2 under control if I have to fight.".

There's fear in his voice and that's enough to make me get up and shift. No, I think I shift first and then get up. It's all a bit fuzzy, but the sense of danger drives me forward, out of the lab and into the corridor. They're coming. Down the steps, through the doors. There they are. Twenty men that smell of sweet catnip. I want to drink them dry, but first I need to protect my family.

I sprint, my feet barely touching the ground, until I

reach the first of them. They aim their weapons at me, but everything is in slow motion. Well, they are slow and I'm in motion. I'm fast. I dive beneath their blades, ripping out one throat after another. My claws disembowel and cut through flesh, while my jaws break bones with delightful cracks. One after the next, their heartbeats stop. Some start again before I get the chance to rip off their hands, but they don't have long enough to heal. Eventually, they'll all be dead.

A few of their blades nick my skin, but I don't even feel the pain. I'm stronger than any of them and so much faster. I'm a predator and they're my prey. They should realise that and lay down their weapons, but they're far too stupid. They weren't created to think. They were made to be my food source. Something about that thought strikes me as important, but I don't have the time to ponder on it. I have more lives to take, more throats to rip out, more blood to drink.

By the time my sisters join me, there are only two left. I turn and let them deal with the two men. Call it being nice and giving them the chance to have some fun. Instead, I run to the rest of my family. Gryphon is standing by the door to the lab, with my other sister closely behind him. She smells strange. I didn't realise that earlier, but there's something very off about her scent. It's like mine but twisted, as if someone took a beautiful melody and added dissonances and notes that don't belong. I rub against Gryphon's legs, encouraging him to give me a good head rub. He complies, but only strokes me in a small spot between my ears and not all over how I want it.

"You should clean up first," he tells me. "You're covered in blood, and I think that's a piece of colon on your back."

Grudgingly, I sit down and start licking my fur. The blood doesn't taste quite as good as when it's straight from the vein, but I still enjoy it. Behind me, the heartbeats have fallen silent. My sisters have killed the two remaining mutants. Good girls. They're coming back towards me, followed by more footsteps. Ryker and Lennox. I recognise them immediately. They're accompanied by the light-footed pawsteps of several cats.

The speaker in the lab makes a buzzing sound before a familiar voice returns. "I'm almost impressed. Maybe we should have given you these quantities of B4 blood before. It's certainly got a fascinating effect."

"Do you know him?" Gryphon whispers.

"No," Ivy says at the same time as her sister mutters, "Maybe."

"No," I meow, a loud rumble that the others likely won't understand.

Gryphon pets my head absentmindedly. Finally. Maybe I need to growl more to get my cuddles from him.

Ryker and Lennox burst into the lab, followed by lots of cats. Some of them have blood on their fur; they must have seen some action too.

Ryker stares at the pile of bodies on the floor. "You've been busy. Who made the mess outside? Kat, I presume?"

I grin at him, exposing my sharp teeth. He presumes correctly.

"She's stoned," Gryphon explains. "Too much blood. We need to get her out of here before she does something stupid."

I growl. I may be a little fuzzy, but I can recognise an insult when I hear one.

He ignores me. "And that's K2. I've tamed her with my siren song for now, so she's safe to be around. What have you found downstairs?"

Lennox shrugs. "Lots of boring storage rooms. A couple of mutants tried to stop us, but that wasn't much of a problem. We were about to come upstairs anyway when Eiryss came to fetch us."

The large tabby meows proudly when her name is mentioned.

"Such a lovely reunion." The voice from the speaker is making me angry. I stop licking myself and get to my feet, growling at the speaker. "It's a pity I have to kill you all. I'll be looking forward to doing autopsies on your bodies though. You should be proud; you'll help science tremendously."

I hiss and run to the door, jumping as high as I can, just about reaching the speaker. My claws sink into the metal and rip it apart. The speaker lands on the floor with a satisfying crash, together with little pieces of wall. Oops.

"Thanks Kat, I was close to doing the same." Lennox grins. "That guy was talking too much. Shall we continue our exploration?"

To be fair, I'd much prefer to stay here and relax, close to all the bleeding bodies who're waiting to be drunk dry. I'm no longer hungry, but there's always room for dessert.

Suddenly, a click comes from the doors.

Ryker runs over and pulls the handle. "They're locked!"

I lazily trot to the doors. They won't be a match for me. I'm stronger than a set of lifeless doors. They don't even have claws.

Before I get to throw myself at them, a hissing sound makes me look up at the ceiling. Blue smoke is streaming into the room through little valves that I thought were for water to rain down in case of a fire.

"Gas!" Gryphon shouts. "We need to get out of here."

Lennox pulls some lock picks from a hidden pocket near his collar. I like how he puts his picks and darts in the same place I do. It creates a sort of bond between us. He runs to the doors and goes on his knees, getting to work with trying to open the lock. I still think I should just attack the doors and be done with it, but for some reason, the others don't agree with my plan.

The smoke is now covering the entire ceiling and is slowly drifting down. It's slow, but it'll be reaching us soon. In the face of danger, my mind clears a little. We need to get out. Yes, Gryphon already said that, but it's taken me a while to really understand his words.

Ryker coughs. "Not sure what this is but I doubt it's good. Wrap some cloth around your mouth."

And then he takes off his shirt and rips it to pieces. I could have helped him with that. His bare chest makes my mouth water. He's gorgeous and totally lickable. I'm kind of hoping that his shirt won't be enough and he'll have to take off his trousers too.

He hands out strips of his shirt and they all follow his lead, knotting it around their head so that their lower half of the face is covered. They all look like bandits now. They've forgotten K2 though, who's standing away from the group, her face blank.

I rip the last remaining piece of cloth from Ryker's hand and walk over to K2. She doesn't react. Stupid sister.

"Good thinking." Gryphon takes the fabric from me and wraps it around K2's mouth and nose. "Lennox, any progress with the door?"

"No, it's got some kind of mechanism that constantly changes. Whenever I'm close to unlocking it, it transforms. I'm trying to discern some kind of pattern, but I've not found one yet."

"Hurry up," Ryker coughs. The smoke is now low enough to reach their heads.

They all crouch low, even K2 after Gryphon tells her to do it. She's like a puppet whose strings need to be pulled for every single thing.

I prowl around the room, impatient for Lennox to finally open those doors. The blue fog is giving me the creeps. Maybe I should have some more blood to steady my nerves. Yes, that feels like a good idea. I choose the closest corpse and lap up some of the blood still trickling from his neck. The head is somewhere else, so it's a bit like blood from the tap. As soon as it runs down my throat, the world turns happier. Colours are brighter. The lab is beautiful. And that smoke…gorgeous.

"Oh no, she's had more blood," Ivy groans, followed by several coughs. "Is she always this stupid when she's shifted?"

I growl and expose my canines menacingly. Blood drips from the fur on my face. Such a waste.

"I don't feel so good." Four sits down on the floor, her face pale behind the cloth.

"Lennox, hurry up!" Gryphon shouts. "This stuff is poisoning us."

I have enough. I run to the doors and throw myself against them, just about managing to avoid crashing into Lennox. They don't budge. I snarl and do it again, and again. The metal groans under my onslaught but the doors hold.

"It's no use. Let me continue with the lock picks," Lennox says, coughs interrupting his words.

I look around the room. The others are all on the floor, pale and moving slowly. The gas is affecting them severely. I don't feel any different though. Maybe it's because I'm shifted. I run to Ryker and nudge his leg.

"Shift," I order.

Luckily, he understands me. "I can't. I tried. Whatever they're poisoning us with is stopping me from shifting."

"Same for us," Ivy coughs weakly. Her eyes flutter shut. Her sister is already unconscious and the others are close to fainting as well. Their coughs are getting weaker.

Fuck. This is bad. I need to do something. I'm the only one still functioning. They're relying on me.

Suddenly, my mind is crystal clear. I know what to do.

CHAPTER TEN

Their heartbeats are getting weaker and their breathing shallow. The gas is killing my family, my friends. Even the cats are affected, meowing pitifully as they huddle together as if being together will somehow save them.

Lennox slowly sinks to the ground, crumpling into a heap. I nudge him with my paw, but he doesn't react. Fuck. I need to act now before it's too late.

The wall to the right of the doors is covered in shelving, but it doesn't take me long to demolish them, revealing the wall behind. When I destroyed the speaker, I saw how brittle the wall was. If I'm lucky, it's weak enough for me to break through.

I step back and draw on all the strength I possess. I'm glad I drank all that blood now. I feel stronger than ever before.

I run, jump and crash into the wall, my claws leaving deep marks in the plaster. It hurts, but I do it again, and again. With every time, more bits of cement fall to the floor. I think I've broken a rib or two, judging from the agony in my side, but I don't stop. I will heal.

I tear at the wall. A sharp pain shoots through my left paw. Fuck, I broke a claw, but there, next to where it's embedded in the plaster, is a tiny hole. Finally. Using my right paw like a human fist, I punch the wall – and it crumbles in a cloud of dust. Fresh air hits me and I breathe in deep. And cough because of all the dust. Very clever, Kat.

I push against the edges of the hole with all my strength, widening it further until it's big enough for me to walk through without my fur getting caught on the ragged edges. Lennox was the last to pass out, so he's the first I drag out of the lab by carefully wrapping my jaws around his leg. I can't avoid piercing his skin with my sharp teeth, but better for him to have some puncture marks than being dead.

I drag him halfway down the corridor where the air is clear. If I'm lucky, he'll recover fast enough to help me with the others. Then I run back into the lab, where the blue fumes are making it hard to see. I listen for their heartbeats. The cats are worst off, their little hearts close to stopping. I manage to grab three of them by the scruffs of their necks, like a mother her kittens, and carry them out. It takes me five runs until all the cats are evacuated. By the time I drop the last batch near Lennox, he's moving ever so slightly. Good, he's recovering. It seems the effect of the gas doesn't last long once you're out of its reach.

Four is next to be dragged out. Her heart is fluttering weakly. I keep waiting for it to stop; she's that poorly.

When I gently lay her next to Lennox, he's already sitting up, looking dazed but no longer as pale.

"How did you-" His eyes fall on the hole in the wall. "Oh."

I grin at him, but there's no time to linger. I run back and forth until Ivy, K2 and Gryphon are all outside. Lennox takes off their cloth masks and helps them sit up when they slowly awake from their poison-induced sleep.

Ryker is last. His heartbeat seemed the strongest when I decided in which order to get them out, but just when I clamp my jaws around his upper arm, his breathing stops and one second later, his heart beats for the final time. Panic floods my mind. He's dead. I need to help him, but he won't be able to be revived here among the poison.

I grip his arm and pull him outside as fast as I can. His body bumps against tables and chairs, but I don't care. As soon as I've got him out of the room, I shift. I shouldn't be able to, not after such a short time and all that energy I expended, but it's instinctual. It hurts, but that's nothing against the pain in my heart as I look at his lifeless face.

I gently bend back his head and pinch his nose shut before pressing my mouth against his. I give him my breath, my life; I'd give anything to get him back.

Another breath, then I lay my hands on his chest and start compressions. We were taught CPR at the Pack, along with extensive first aid. Assassins get hurt a lot. This is the first time I've actually had to do it in real life. The Pack turned us into solitary killers who rarely worked together, so I was never there when one of us got killed. If I could, I'd go back and kill lots of people, just to practice CPR on them.

Two more breaths. His lips are growing cold.

More chest compressions.

I dimly notice the others approaching, but I keep my focus on Ryker.

One. Two. Three. Four. Five.

Please, Ryker. Wake up.

My mouth on his. Breathe. Breathe.

His chest lifts, but that's only because I'm giving him my own air.

Come on, Ryker, you can do this. Don't leave me.

One. Two. Ba-bumm. His heart beats. Then stops again. But it beat on its own accord, that gives me hope. Three. Four. Five.

Ba-bumm. Ba-bumm.

It keeps beating and then he takes his first rattling breath. I could kiss him for doing this. He's a fighter and now he's battled death and won. Not many people can say the same.

Lennox puts his hands on my shoulders and I let myself fall back against his legs. I'm exhausted. The adrenaline is rapidly disappearing, leaving me tired and aching all over. My left side is the worst. I wish we could go home now to recover, but we don't have that luxury. I have a scientist to find and kill. With some torture in between. Oh yes, he's going to suffer.

Gryphon stays with K2, Ryker and most of the cats. Ryker is still unconscious but his heart is beating steadily once more. I hate having to leave him like that, but I know that Gryphon will do all he can to look after my favourite cat, even though he's still injured himself. As soon as Ryker wakes up, they're to leave the building and return home. I wish we could search the lab, but the blue smoke is still pouring from the ceiling. We've moved Ryker to the very end of the corridor where he's far away from the fumes, and if the fog spreads, Gryphon will have K2 to help him carry Ryker somewhere safer.

Lennox, the twins and I return to the stairwell and go up to the next floor. It looks exactly like the one below. Rows and rows of small offices with large double doors at the end. Let's hope the entire building isn't all like that. It will take forever to search every room. Luckily, we're not human and have excellent senses at our disposal.

"There's someone above us," Ivy whispers.

I listen as hard as I can. "Three people," I say after a moment. "Two of them mutants."

By now, I'm pretty adept at telling them apart from other species. Their heartbeats are faster, but their breathing is a little slower than that of humans or shifters.

"Let's hope that's the guy we're looking for." Lennox rubs the back of his neck. "I'm debating whether to shift. Ripping his throat out seems more satisfying than poking him with knives."

Four pulls a little vial from her pocket. "I suggest poison. It seems fitting."

I take it from her and give it a sniff. Sundried apples with a hint of fennel. "Daughter's Revenge?"

She shrugs. "One of my favourites. Slow and painful."

"I know, I've used it a couple of times. Not the most elegant of poisons, but it's certainly effective. Let's make him talk first though. He's no use to us when he's foaming on the mouth or missing his throat."

Lennox chuckles. "Finally you're talking sense. Did the poison make you sane again?"

I elbow him in the ribs. "No, you being in danger did."

"I think you're going to have to explain what happened there, later," Four complains. "You should have told us about your little problem beforehand."

"My little problem?" I scoff. "I don't have a problem."

"Getting stoned on the blood of the dead isn't a problem?" She puts her hands on her hips, glaring at me. "You endangered us all with your behaviour."

I bare my teeth before I can control myself. "How many more brutes than you did I kill? Twenty-five, maybe? So be quiet and stop complaining."

She purses her lips but doesn't respond.

I ignore her and start heading up the stairs to the floor where the three people are hiding. This one doesn't have the same layout as the two storeys below. Yes, there's another corridor, but glass doors lead to open meeting rooms, not tiny office cubicles. At the end of the hallway are the familiar double doors, but they're open.

Not another lab, I hope. I really want a change of scenery. And no more poison.

The heartbeats lead me to one of the doors on the right. The others are close behind me, their weapons drawn. My knives at the ready, I step towards the frosted glass door. I can't look through it, but I can hear their breathing inside. Definitely the people we're looking for.

"Ready," Lennox whispers.

I nod and without further ado, storm into the room. I take in the scene in a flash. Two grunts protectively guarding a blond man. He seems familiar, but I don't have time to think about where I might have seen him before. Is he the one who talked to us through the speakers? I need to hear his voice to make sure.

The grunts don't attack, so I don't either. I want to know what this is all about first before I gut them.

"You shouldn't be alive," the man says. Yes, it's him. His voice sounds older than he looks. His blond hair falls to just above his grey eyes. He's attractive in a very siren way. I'm sure women would love to spend the night with him if they got the chance. Men, too. He wears a slim fitting black suit, unlike the two grunts who're in tight t-shirts and jeans. That seems to be their uniform here.

"Well, we are. Now who are you?"

I resist giving him a snarl. I don't want to appear too feral - for now. Until I get to torture him. I'm really looking forward to that.

"I'd rather you stay in the dark. We put a lot of effort into erasing your memories. It would be a pity to change that."

I launch myself forward, faster than ever, and embed

my knives in the necks of the two grunts. They fall to the ground and before they can recover, the twins are by my side, cutting off one head each. I give them an appreciative nod. We're a good team.

The man wipes some blood splatters from his pretty face. "That wasn't necessary."

I laugh at him. "Oh, it really was. Now, I'm asking one last time, who are you?"

"Someone interested in you. Very interested. In fact, I've been following the three of you ever since I started my career as one of Professor Lakefield's students."

Now I know where I've seen him before. That other scientist showed me pictures when I was his captive. One of them was a blond man, a younger version of this siren.

"How come we don't remember you?" I ask him, twirling my knives in my hands as a gentle nudge of encouragement.

"Because we've made you forget. We conditioned you to forget all the little inconvenient moments we had with you. It was important especially for you, K1, to not make you feel like a lab rat. By erasing your memories of all the tests and experiments we did on you, it always felt like the first time for you. It helped us establish a baseline and then see your reactions change depending on what we did to you."

"But what is it that you actually did?" I'm almost shouting now. I'm so close to answers, but it feels like I have to dig for every single one. Why can't it just be easy for one fucking time in my life?

"That would be telling." He chuckles but sneers at me at the same time. "Shall we play a game?"

"I remember him saying that," Four whispers.

The siren turns to her. "You remember, my little angel? What do you recall of our meetings?"

Little angel? I want to punch him in the face. Four curls her hands into fists, clearly having the same urge.

"I don't," she snaps. "But I want you to tell me what you did to me. To us. You owe that to us."

He laughs. "I owe you? No, I don't think so. You've been nothing but trouble. Escaping from our care, killing my people, and now you've gone on a rampage in my last remaining lab. That doesn't endear you to me, you understand? If you want me to talk, then I need certain assurances."

Does he actually think we'd let him live? Well, if he wants, he can believe that. It's not going to happen though. I'm going to kill him as soon as I have my answers.

"I promise to let you go once you've told us everything," I lie. I'm a good liar, but he doesn't buy it.

"Nice try. I want one of you as my guarantee that you'll let me live. One of you, collared. I'll release her once I'm out of the city and you can come and find her."

"No way," I snarl. "You'll never put a collar on one of us ever again. But maybe I should put one on you? What would happen?"

His expression doesn't change, but his heartbeat increases. Interesting. He's scared of that.

I grin. "Lennox, would you mind finding us a collar?"

"At your service." He laughs softly and leaves the room. I keep forgetting that Lennox has a grudge to settle with the Pack as well. He may not have been cloned and experimented on, but he was their prisoner for most of his childhood. They abused him, turned him into a killer. Who knows what kind of person he might have become if he'd grown up away from the Pack.

"You can't put a collar on me," the siren protests. "It's not going to work."

I step closer until I'm eye to eye with him. "Are you sure about that? Really, really sure?"

He blinks, telling me all I need to know.

"Talk. This is your last chance. Start with your name."

"Shaun," he says with a sigh. "Shaun Jayden."

That doesn't sound like a name for a murderous psychopathic scientist, but I guess we can't choose our names. Our parents do that. Or the evil scientists who created us, in my case.

"What is your role here, Shaun?" I ask.

"I'm in charge of Project Indigo."

I groan. "From now on, I want you to answer with lots of detail. I'm not going to pull every fricking answer from your miserable mouth."

He smirks. "You've turned out so well. In some ways. In others, you've been an utter failure."

I ignore him. "What's Project Indigo?"

"The future. Not just for shifters, but for all of us. Sirens, succubi, otherworldly creatures. We'll be the ones ruling the world. Right now, we work in the shadows, but with the powers that Indigo can bestow upon us, that will change."

"What powers?" I ask, dreading the answer.

"Yours. A little improved, of course. K9 and K10 were almost perfect. You were the prototype, so we can't really expect you to fulfil the brief."

"And what's that brief?" Ivy interrupts.

"Strength. Agility. Healing ability. Endurance. Intelligence. Obedience."

I laugh at the last word. "Now I know why I failed."

He glares at me. "You shouldn't sound so proud of that. You may have been allowed to live a little longer if you'd been more subservient."

"Allowed?" I repeat. "I don't need anybody's permission to live. That's just...crazy. You're crazy." I take a deep breath before I lose my composure. "What does the drug do?"

"What drug?"

I pull one of the vials from my pocket. Thank goodness for my strange shifter magic that allows me to keep on my clothes including everything that's in my pockets.

"This drug. We know you've been giving it to us. Why?"

"Take it and find out." He meets my eyes defiantly. "Or are you scared?"

"Why would I subject myself to that when I can just force you to talk?" I counter. "You gave us this drug to make us into your perfect weapons. That's what this is about, right? Transforming us into soldiers you can use to stay in power?"

"You're thinking way too small," he snickers. "We're not just planning to produce more of you. We're planning to turn everyone into you. That's the next step of the project. Labs in other cities are working on it already. Just because you destroyed ours doesn't mean this ends here. My death won't change anything. We're everywhere and we're going to win."

I really want to punch him, but that would set a bad example to my sisters. Their tension is visible; they're holding back attacking him.

"Trust me, you don't want everyone to be like me, like us. We make very bad slaves."

He chuckles. "I believe you've met K2? If everyone was like her, we'd have both excellent workers and fantastic soldiers. She doesn't need a collar; she does whatever we want. Conditioned to respond to sirens only. Which is why she's currently attacking your friends."

CHAPTER ELEVEN

I run out of the room, trusting the twins to look after Shaun Jayden. And when I say 'look after', I mean hurt and torture. That man is evil through and through.

Lennox passes me on the stairs, holding a collar. "Put that on him and make him pay," I shout as I run past him, taking two steps at a time.

Gryphon and the others are no longer in the corridor where we left them. That means they're on their way home. Oh no. I sprint through the empty entrance hall and out into the night. Clouds have pulled over the stars like a blanket, making it seem gloomier than before. I follow my friends' scent. They didn't take the route via the roofs this time; they're walking along the roads. I'm amazed Ryker is well enough to walk already, but maybe Gryphon is carrying him. Ryker was dead, after all. Completely dead. My heart aches at the thought. I can't lose him. He's way too precious to me. I realise that now. I should have before. When we're back home, safe and away from all the trouble, I'm going to tell him.

Screams in the distance make me run even faster. I'm tempted to shift, but I might be of more use as a human. Besides, I no longer trust my body to behave as I'm used to. I might end up stuck in one shape or half-shifted. So I stay human, but draw from my new strength as much as I can to propel me forward with more energy.

I cross a corner and carnage lies before me. Ryker is on the floor, lifeless, again. Gryphon is fighting K2, his sword blazing through the air, while three cats are clawing at my sister's legs. Storm is on Ryker's chest, her fur standing in all directions, her back arched. She's ready to defend her family. Good kitty. But now I'm here.

"K2!" I shout as loud as I can. "Come and fight me."

Not that I really want to do that, but Gryphon looks exhausted and he needs a break. Maybe he can regain control of her once he doesn't have to fight for his life.

K2 looks at me blankly and for a moment, I'm not sure if she's going to take the bait. But then she growls and starts running at me, her hands turned into claws once more. She doesn't need a weapon with those blades on her hands. I don't want to hurt her, but she has no such inhibitions. I draw my knives and take on a defensive stance. Hurry up, Gryphon, stop her. With a feral growl, she leaps into the air, her claws pointed at me. I roll to one side, just about evading her attack. She hisses as she lands and crouches low, like a cat about to jump.

"Stop it, we can help you. You don't have to fight me."

She doesn't react to my words at all. Not that I thought she would, but it was worth a try. She attacks again and I deflect her claws with my knives without going in the offensive. Again and again, I evade her by dropping to the ground or rolling aside. She's getting frustrated, but I'm not going to attack her. This is just playing for time. Out of the corner of my eye, I see Gryphon moving towards us. I hope that means he's about to try and get her under control again. I'm not sure how much longer I can hold her off. With each time I deflect her attack, she gets angrier. Spittle flies from her mouth as I dance around her, keeping a safe distance from her claws. She could skewer me with those. I wonder if they hurt her. They're longer than even my panther claws and that means something. Shaun Jayden was right, she's a formidable weapon. Fighting one of her is bad enough, and I really don't want to imagine there being an army of her. Nobody would be safe. Yet more reason to stop the Pack and the sirens.

Gryphon starts to sing and immediately, I feel a little lighter. Like a burden has been taken off me. The melody soothes and embraces me, gently touching my heart. I want to lean into it, close my eyes and let it seep into my soul, but K2 is still trying to fight me. She's getting slower though and her eyes are no longer as focused. Gryphon's song is having an effect on her, but it's not enough to stop her. Fuck. I bet that's the scientist's doing. He must have some kind of hold on her, one that's stronger than Gryphon's. No idea how he manages to do that from this distance, but it's enough to make K2 keep attacking me. The song makes me slower too, not just her, and this time, I don't evade her fast enough. Her claws slash open my arm and blood spurts from the wound. I cry out in pain and stumble backwards, clutching my arm. The gashes are deep; I think I can see bone. I'm going to kill Shaun for that. He made my sister wound me. That's unforgivable.

Gryphon's song is getting louder, taking away some of the pain. K2 puts her hands on her ears, probably trying to stop the music from influencing her, but luckily, Gryphon is strong. She stops moving, frozen in place, her claws still pointing at me. He keeps singing and I can almost understand the words that are binding her in place, wrapping around her like ropes. I'd feel pity if I wasn't in so much pain.

He ends the music with a beautiful low note that makes my entire chest open, then rushes to my side. "How bad is it?"

"It's deep but nothing I can't handle. Do you have some of those cloth pieces left?"

He hands me a strip of the shirt and helps me wrap it around the wound. I wince whenever he touches it. Blood immediately seeps through the fabric, but that's nothing that can be helped. I need to get back to the twins and let Ivy lick my arm. I cringe at the thought. That skill really is a little disgusting. Not that I don't like licking people, but... anyway.

"You should sit down, you're all pale." Gryphon gently puts his hands on my shoulders and physically forces me to sit. He probably knows that I wouldn't have done it otherwise.

"I need to get back," I protest. "We found the guy in charge. I need answers. He was starting to give us information but then said he'd taken control of K2. What happened?"

"I'd stopped keeping a proper hold on her," he says with a regretful sigh. "I thought she was secure, especially after we'd left the building. She was walking alongside us, not giving us any trouble, so I let my guard slip. Suddenly, her claws grew and she started attacking. She didn't say a word, just slashed at me. I dropped Ryker to defend myself, but it's good that you showed up when you did. She was getting the upper hand. Fighting without wanting to injure really isn't fun."

"Tell me about it. When this is over, we need to do a proper assassination together. Some good old killing without holding back."

"Deal."

Gryphon sits down by my side. Beads of sweat line his forehead. He got injured earlier, I mustn't forget that. We all need some rest and time to recover. But not yet. If only my arm weren't hurting this much. It's making it hard to concentrate. I need to make a plan for what to do next, but the pain is clouding my mind. I much preferred the catnip-blood induced mind fog earlier.

"I can go back," Gryphon suggests. "We can tie up K2 or even knock her out. I don't think you should go back there. You're far too pale. I'll get the twins to come to you and help you."

I shake my head. "No, I need to do this. I need to

talk to the scientist and get my answers. It's just a scratch, it's not going to kill me."

"That's not a scratch." He scoffs. "Has anyone ever told you not to carry the whole world on your shoulders?"

"Nope. Because I'm not doing that. I'm a cat, I'm selfish. I don't care about the world. All I want is to be happy and warm and fed."

I'm cold, I realise that now. The coldness is starting in my arm and is slowly permeating through the rest of my body. I carefully unwrap the cloth from my wound. Fuck.

Gryphon gasps. "That looks like poison."

It does indeed. Dark blue lines circle the wound like a spider's web. The edges of the gashes are turning dark and strangely dry. It doesn't look like any of the poisons I'm familiar with."

"Can you make her talk?" I ask. "Tell us what this is?"

"I'll try." He gets up and walks over to K2, who's still standing there, frozen.

He hums a simple melody and it washes over me like a warm wind. Nothing as elaborate or deep as his usual song, but K2 starts to move into a more natural position and looks up at him.

The humming turns into a song, the words not meant for me.

"I don't know," she suddenly says, her voice so monotonous it's almost robotic.

Gryphon continues the song; it becomes fuller, more detailed. It gives me the urge to tell him something, a secret, but I don't know what. It's hard to resist his song even though he's trying to make K2 talk and not me.

"It's in me. I don't know the name. I don't know if there's an antidote."

She may be answering Gryphon's questions, but I'm not happy about the answers at all. No antidote. Fuck that. Of course there's one. The Pack researchers wouldn't want to be around a shifter with poisonous claws unless they had a way to reverse any damage she might do to them.

"Ask her if she's ever injured someone at the lab," I tell the siren.

He nods and his song changes slightly.

"Yes, many times."

Go, girl! I just wish she'd talk in a normal voice and not sound like a machine.

"And did you see them again after that?"

It takes a moment for Gryphon to translate my question into his music. I wish she'd just answer me directly, but that doesn't seem to be possible. We're going to have to find a better way to communicate with her once we're home. It can't stay like that.

"Yes."

I sigh in relief. That means there's a cure. Now, all we need to do is find it.

A groan makes me turn around. Ryker is moving, trying to sit up. Before I can even consider getting up myself, the cats are swarming around him, purring, rubbing against his side. He's surrounded by cats and has never looked sexier.

I try to get to my feet and check on him, but

dizziness overwhelms me and I sink back to the ground, barely managing to stay in a sitting position. I feel like lying down. My arm feels like it's been stuck in a freezer. Goosebumps are spreading over my skin. I really don't like this poison. It's not very elegant. I was given a lot of different poisons at the Pack - they were of the opinion that you only knew the true effects of a poison until you'd experienced them yourself - but this time, there's no one standing next to me with the antidote. It's no fun being on this side of the poisoning process.

"Kat, don't try and get up," Gryphon says sharply, hurrying towards me.

"Too late," I mutter tiredly. "Tried and failed."

He runs his hands through his hair. "I don't know what to do. You can't go back, but if I go, K2 might get out of control again. If I take her with me, the siren in the lab could find it even easier to wrestle her from me. Ryker isn't well enough. We can't send the cats either because nobody will understand them-"

"Wrong. My sisters will."

He looks at me with a concerned frown. "Are you sure?"

No, I'm not. I've not seen them interact with any of the cats. They don't seem to have the natural affinity I feel for my fellow felines, but they're like me, right? They should understand the cats.

I rummage through my pockets until I find a tiny pen and a crumpled piece of paper. I always carry those with me. You never know when you might have to write a ransom note.

I try to scribble a message, but my hand is shaking

way too much. The cold has taken over my entire body now and I'm shivering from top to bottom. Even my teeth are starting to chatter.

"Let me," Gryphon says gently and pulls the pen from my hand. He writes a few words on the paper, then folds it. "Which cat should be the messenger?"

"Storm, come here!" I call.

The black cat looks at me for a moment, clearly preferring to stay with Ryker, but he gives her a gentle nudge and she trots over.

"I need you to run back to the lab and give this to Lennox. As fast as you can, please."

She rubs her head against my hand in acknowledgement. Gryphon hands her the piece of paper and she carefully takes it in her mouth. I hope it won't be covered in cat saliva by the time Lennox gets it.

She runs off, disappearing into the night. She's swallowed up by the darkness, and I really hope that's not a metaphor for something.

I feel like I'm being swallowed by coldness. Sitting upright is becoming a struggle, but I don't want to appear weak in front of the guys. Gryphon seems to sense my predicament and sits by my side, putting an arm around my shoulders and pulling me against him. I let go, using him as my pillar of support.

Ryker has managed to sit up, pale but alive. I wish I could go over, or have him come here so that I can be sandwiched between the two men, but I'm far too weak, and so is he. Only a few yards separate us, but it feels like miles.

"I'm so cold," I whisper, before a wave of darkness

comes out of nowhere and overwhelms me. I float away on a river of ice, drifting towards an end I didn't see coming.

CHAPTER TWELVE

In an ideal world, I would have awoken in a warm bed surrounded by my family.

Sadly, this isn't an ideal world.

The ground is hard and cold beneath me and stones are poking into my back. I almost wish I was unconscious again. But wait, how am I back in the land of the living?

I open my eyes - and stare into my own. I blink. It's not a mirror, nor is it one of the twins.

K2.

I try to get up and preferably as far away from her as possible, but my body refuses to budge.

She stares at me, her gaze boring into mine, but she's not attacking. I allow myself to relax again, although I keep up my guard. K2 is too unpredictable not to.

"We need to talk," she says, her voice no longer robotic. It almost sounds like my own, but a little deeper with a trace of a lisp.

"Where are the others?"

"I'm here." Gryphon steps into my field of view. "Lennox has taken Ryker home, helped by the twins. And all the cats. They got in the way more than they helped, but that wasn't to be avoided. They're very protective of him."

Alright, I'm on my own with Gryphon and K2. And she's talking normally. My head swirls with questions. I start with the most obvious one.

"What the fuck is going on?"

"We need to talk," K2 repeats. "Now."

"She's right. I'm not sure how long I can keep her like this."

"Like a person?" I ask just to make sure.

She hisses and I can't help but flinch. I'm in the most vulnerable position possible, with an aggressive cat shifter on top of me. Not used to that.

"We only have a few minutes," she snaps. Not a ray of sunshine behind her serial killer persona then. I'm not surprised. "Doctor Jayden's death has released me from the siren net, but it's closing in already. Gryphon is holding it open, but he's not got enough experience."

"Death?" I repeat. "He's dead?"

"The twins," Ryker explains. "But don't worry, they found out quite a few things."

"Quiet," K2 hisses.

"I've not felt this clear in years. There's something you need to know. They can do this to you too. We're all the same. You can't let them close. If you let them give you the drug again, they'll get into your mind."

"This drug?" I take one of the vials from my pocket, amazed it's not broken.

She sniffs the air and anger flashes across her face. "Yes. Destroy it. If you take it often enough, they turn you into theirs. It weakens your barriers, makes you vulnerable. And it twists your connection with your cat."

Her anger morphs into sadness. Regret.

"Is that why your claws are like that?"

K2 nods. "It's the only thing I have left of her. They've forced everything else into my human body. The strength, the endurance."

I stare at her in shock. "You can no longer shift?"

"I can't keep her for much longer," Gryphon warns sharply.

"You need to kill me," K2 says as simply as if she was talking about the weather or telling me that the night is dark. "I can't take this any longer."

"You're free now. We can find a way to make you better."

She laughs harshly. "There is no way. I welcome death. I've craved it for years, whenever I've had a lucid moment. They've become rare, but I do still have them, sometimes. They forbid me to kill myself; otherwise I would have long since done it, especially after what I did to the twins."

True regret shines in her eyes. Her sorrow makes me feel cold inside and this time, it's got nothing to do with poison.

"No. I can't do that. But I promise you we'll help you. I've got friends who're great with science. They'll find an antidote to the drug they've given you."

K2 shakes her head. "There's no hope for me, trust

me. They told me how they tried to reverse the effects of the drug in other clones. They all died. It's permanent."

Suddenly, she cringes and for a moment, her eyes go blank. She blinks, twice, then her expression is back to normal, animated rather than static, but it's clear that she's fading.

"Please," she begs, no longer as tough as she appeared earlier. "You have to do it. It has to be you."

"No," I repeat. "I can't."

"Then I will try and kill you. Your siren won't always have control of me. As soon as he loses it, I'll be attacking you and the other clones. It's what I'm programmed to do. I can't fight it. It's you or me, sunshine."

"Sisters."

"What?"

"I call them my sisters. Not clones. And you're my sister too. I'm not going to kill one of my own."

She stares at me as if I've said something confusing.

"Sisters?"

"Yes. Family. We're the same, yet we do have our differences. We may have been created rather than born, but that doesn't mean we can't be like people. I've made my own family. Mates, sisters, friends. And you can be part of it."

"Almost gone," Gryphon groans, visibly struggling. I don't really understand the whole siren thing, but it's clear that he's not going to be able to hold on for much longer.

"We'll help you," I say once more. "Do you have a name?"

Again, she stares at me in confusion. "K2," she mutters after a pause. "But you know that already."

"I meant a real name. One that doesn't contain a number. I know K1 and Kat are kind of similar, but that's just a coincidence. My full name is Katriona. How about you come up with one too? One that you can make your own. A new start to a new life."

A tiny smile curves her lips. "That would be nice."

Gryphon cries out and I turn to look at him, but he's fine, just looking extremely exhausted. When I look back at K2, her expression is completely gone once more. She's a robot again.

Flaring hate fills me. The Pack have done this to her. I thought they'd done bad things to Little Kat, the twins and me, but this trumps it all. The worst part is that she has lucid moments. She's aware of her predicament and can't do anything about it.

I reach out and stroke her cheek. Of course she doesn't respond at all, but I'd like to imagine that she can feel it, somehow.

Gryphon hums a few notes and she steps back, giving him space to kneel by my side.

"How are you feeling?"

I smile up at him. "Alive."

"Good. Then let's get you home and keep it that way."

ON THE WAY BACK TO THE WAGON, GRYPHON FILLS ME IN on what happened.

The collar Lennox put around Shaun Jayden's neck worked. Not quite as expected though. It turned him into a very friendly, very helpful man who was only too happy to show them where the antidote for my poison was hidden. He also answered all the questions Lennox and the twins put to him. Gryphon doesn't know much about that, so I'm going to have to wait until we're back home to find out. Doctor Jayden even gave them files containing everything about Project Indigo.

Annoyingly, the collar also had the side effect of exploding the doctor's head after a couple of minutes. I laugh when Gryphon mentions that. How sad. While it's disappointing that I didn't get to torture and kill the man myself, it's a satisfying ending. Death by exploded head. Brilliant. Life does have a sense of humour after all.

"There were bits of brain on Four's shirt," Gryphon chuckles. "I don't know why the twins wear white clothes, it's so impractical."

"I've been thinking that all night. They must love doing the washing. Maybe we should give them our clothes too." I look at my blood-stained suit, ripped in several places. One sleeve has fallen victim to K2's slashing. "Not sure I can salvage this one though."

My wound has closed and no longer looks as bad. It still needs some proper cleaning and dressing when we're back home, but the effects of the poison are gone now. My body is warm again and while I'm not quite feeling strong, I'm at least no longer as weak. I think it's mostly exhaustion catching up with me. I need to sleep. We all do.

K2 follows behind us, silent and expressionless. I feel

like I should include her in the conversation, but it's no use. She's not herself just now.

"Explain the siren net she mentioned," I ask Gryphon as we make our way through the town. "The way the sirens control her."

"I don't really understand myself. When I control someone with my powers, it feels a bit like a leash that I weave around their mind. I tell them what to do and if they resist, I tighten the leash, increasing the pressure."

"That's not what it feels like to me," I interrupt.

He chuckles. "That's both because I've never tried to force you to do something completely evil and because you're not human. I've been told that humans feel it as a kind of painful suit around their body that moves them around without them able to do anything about it."

Definitely not what I feel when he does it. His music is more like a warm hug, gentle and loving. A caress that's almost intimate.

"Anyway, even if I control several people at once, it's still like I'm holding leashes. I've never felt like having a net nor have I heard any other sirens mention it. I've not been part of siren circles for a while though. My father always pressured me to go to meetings and get more involved, but I took any excuse I could find to avoid that. I don't know how I managed to grow up with a conscience despite being surrounded by power-hungry sirens, but somehow it happened."

I take his hand. "I'm glad. Not that your conscience is that well developed. You wouldn't be enjoying your job otherwise."

He laughs. "That's true. I'd say I have a good moral

compass though. Yes, I kill, but I only kill the bad people. I usually let the good ones run, or only hurt them a tiny bit. For good measure, you know?"

"Yeah, same. How strange that we found each other, two assassins with a conscience."

He stops and squeezes my hand. "Is this the moment where I kiss you?"

I look at K2. "I'm not much into other people watching, especially not someone controlled by sirens."

Gryphon smirks. "Good point. Let's continue this conversation when we're home."

Tickles spread through my belly. Is that what they call butterflies? No, I'm not someone to experience something as pathetic as that. I need to get a grip. I'm acting way too emotional just now. Must be the aftereffects of the poison.

We're close to the wagon now. Finally. I hope the others have already had a shower so that I can claim the bathroom to myself. My skin is covered in blood, both other people's and my own, and luckily I no longer feel the urge to lick it. I don't know what I'd do if a bleeding mutant suddenly fell out of the sky in front of me, so let's not test it. My next fix is going to be catnip, not blood.

CHAPTER THIRTEEN

This time, I really do wake up in a bed. I barely remember falling asleep. I think I sat down on the bed after having a shower, planning to go to the kitchen to get some food, but I must have nodded off.

I stretch and bump against a warm body. I'm surrounded by them. Gryphon, Lennox and Ryker are all on the mattress with me, sleeping in various positions. Ryker is at my feet, curled up like a cat, a soft snore coming from his throat. Adorable.

Gryphon is to my right, on his belly, his chest exposed. Scars run parallel across his back, reminding me of the ones on his face. Like an animal clawed him. I roll to one side and gently run my fingers along one of the scars. His breathing changes; he's awake.

His scars are soft beneath my finger, but they still feel different from his healthy skin. I follow them back and forth, fighting the temptation to lean over and run my tongue over his scars.

I've been with many men, yet their bodies are still a

mystery to me. My own body is hard from training, but there are still soft bits. My boobs, mostly, plus there are always a few wobbly bits around my hips and bum. Not with these men, though. Hard planes meet hard planes. If he turned around, I'd find that even his breast is hard. No man boobs in sight. How can they be so hard yet still have a softness inside that bubbles to the surface whenever they interact with me?

"Do continue," he whispers and I realise I've stopped, having come to the end of the longest of the scars.

"No, my turn." Lennox's voice is husky.

His hot breath kisses my back just before his lips do the same. A pleasant shiver runs over my skin. This is turning into something exciting. The last time we were all in bed like this, I got scared and ran. Now, I want to touch them all. Something's changed, like a switch being flipped inside my head. Maybe it was admitting my worries to them. Maybe it was almost dying. Either way, I want them. Lots.

"Turn onto your back," Lennox whispers.

I oblige, although I regret no longer being able to play with Gryphon's scars.

Both of them are now on their side, staring down at me.

"How much do you like this shirt?" the wolf asks with a cheeky grin.

I have to look down at myself to even know what I'm wearing. I just randomly grabbed something from the wardrobe last night. It's a bland grey t-shirt with some sort of slogan on it. It's not even my own shirt; probably one of Bethany's.

"Not much." My voice has grown hoarse with need. The cat in me is aching to mount the guys and fuck them one by one. Calm down, kitty. Patience.

Lennox grins and his blue eyes glow as he shifts his hand into a wolf's paw. He rips my shirt apart in the middle, exposing my chest, before shifting back into full human.

"I love it when you go all feral." I smile at him. "Do continue with that."

"That dog wouldn't know feral if it hit him in the head," Ryker chuckles, followed by a yawn. "I see you started the party without me. Kat, how much do you like your panties?"

"Copycat," Lennox mutters, but Ryker is already pulling down my panties. At least he's not ripping them. I don't have many of those in the wardrobe.

Gryphon ignores the two shifters and closes in on me, his body pressed to my side. He cups my cheek and makes me turn my head towards him. His lips meet mine in a passionate kiss.

Kissing him is like floating in a sea of catnip. Exhilarating. Beautiful. Overwhelming.

Ryker nudges me to spread my legs. I do so without needing much encouragement. I'm burning to feel him beneath my legs. All of them. I'm greedy today and I'm not going to leave this room until I've had them all.

Soft lips trail a row of kisses along my belly, slowly moving upwards. Lennox. He stops when he reaches my breast and gently swirls his tongue around the base of it.

How can I feel so much from such a small touch? It shouldn't be possible. It's magic, I'm sure of it.

Sparks fly when Ryker's tongue licks my core from top to bottom. He may be human, but his tongue is raspy like that of a cat, making me moan whenever he touches my clit. I spread my legs further, hoping he'll get the hint. I need more. I'm desperate. Moans tumble from my lips and I'm unable to stop them. The more Ryker licks my core, the more I writhe on the bed, shaking, whimpering. It's too much and yet not enough.

Gryphon is still kissing me and I almost feel bad because I can't return his passionate kiss as much as I would like. Too many sensations, not enough brainpower to deal with it.

Lennox suckles on one nipple while twirling the other between his fingers. He teases me with soft kisses all over my breasts, then takes my nub into his mouth again.

I can't bear it.

"Fuck me," I groan against Gryphon's lips.

"Say please," Lennox whispers, gently biting my breast.

I don't want him to be gentle. I want them to go wild and crazy and fuck me like there's no tomorrow.

"Do it or I'll kill you," I hiss. "Now."

Lennox chuckles. "That works too."

Ryker's tongue disappears and I want to complain, but then his cock pushes into me, hard and fast, and I can no longer hold back.

❁ ❁ ❁ ❁ ❁ ❁

I WAKE UP ALONE, SLOW AND GENTLE, BUT THE SCENTS OF the guys are still fresh. I dimly remember waking up when they got up, but I still needed some more sleep, so I ignored them. I pull the duvet closer and breathe in deep. All of their scents combined. I love it. I wish I could wrap myself in the blanket and wear it like a dress. Not that I ever wear dresses. They're not practical attire for an assassin. I tried combining a skirt with leggings once and regretted that when the skirt got caught on a roof tile, almost making me fall. Never again.

I stretch before climbing from our makeshift bed. Just before I'm about to open the door, I realise that I'm naked. Maybe not give my sisters this shock. They're fourteen, so I doubt they're sexually active. I certainly hope not. They're way too messed up to start any relationships anyway.

I smile as I realise how protective I feel about them. Like I want to lock them in a room and never let them out in the real world. Is that what parents feel? If so, then it's amazing that you ever see kids playing out in the street. Mine would probably wear leashes and live in a windowless room just so that they couldn't get in danger. I've seen how evil the world is.

One of the guys left a shirt on the floor, so I put that on, too lazy to rummage through the wardrobe. I only have two sets of panties left in the drawer. Time to find out if my sisters really do like to do the washing. If so, they're going to be my favourite siblings ever. Which reminds me of Little Kat. I should visit her again soon, check up on her. And she might like to meet her older sisters. Not K2, that wouldn't be safe, but the twins should be fine. They're messed up but not a danger per se.

I run my hands through my hair to try and tame my mane, but then, the guys have seen me in a lot more messed up states. Covered in blood and body parts. They'll survive a little frizz.

"Morning," Lily greets me cheerily as soon as I step into the living area. "Eggs?"

I nod. "Starving. Are they safe to eat, though?"

She throws a spoon at me which I catch just before it hits my face. "Totally safe. I can cook, you know."

"Cooking and creating something edible isn't quite the same," I quip. "But yes, I'll take eggs. And tea. And catnip cookies, if you have any."

"We don't. I'm never making those again."

I shrug. "Thought I'd try."

"Catnip cookies?" Four perks up. "Those sound good."

"No," Lily says in her strictest voice. "I'm not being your drug dealer."

"I could provide you with the 'nip," I offer. "You just have to do to the baking. I tried it and…well, you remember what happened."

"She set the kitchen on fire," Lily explains to the twins. "It wasn't pretty. That's why all she's allowed to make is sandwiches. I get worried every time she switches on the kettle."

"Oi, my tea is excellent!"

She snickers. "Except that it's ninety per cent milk with a tiny bit of tea."

"I like milk."

Ivy turns to Bethany, who's in the corner of the bench, reading a magazine. "Are they always like that?"

She nods absentmindedly. "All the time. Their bickering gets a little boring when you live with them."

"I don't think this can get boring," Four grins. "It's like a comedy show."

"You've never been to a show," her sister says with an eyebrow wiggle.

"Yeah, but I'm sure this is what it's like."

I slide onto the bench next to Ryker. He grins at me and puts a hand on my thigh as if that's the most natural thing. He looks entirely like himself again. His yellow eyes sparkle with life and he's no longer pale. It's hard to believe that he was dead last night.

"Sleep well?" he asks innocently.

"Very."

Gryphon laughs. "We could hear that. Your snoring is adorable."

"Not that again. I don't snore. And I'm not adorable. I take great offence at that."

The guys exchange a look. "So adorable," Ryker confirms.

I sigh. They're going to drive me crazy. One is bad enough, but now I'm stuck with three. My sanity is hanging by a thread and they're going to enjoy cutting it.

Lily puts a plate of scrambled eggs in front of me. Not sure they were supposed to be scrambled, but at least they look edible. She throws two slices of toast on top.

I start shovelling the food into me, realising how hungry I really am. I'd planned to eat something when we returned last night, but fell asleep before I ever got the chance.

"Where's Lennox?" I ask in between bites.

"Gone to meet his employer," Gryphon replies while watching me with an amused smile. "Said it had something to do with the wolves you encountered."

Oh. Last time we talked about Lennox's job, he said he'd taken some time off. Will he have to return to work already? I hope not. I like having him around. Maybe, once I've got M.E.O.W. running again, I can convince him to work for me. I've got the cash to pay him at least as much as his current employer. Our last case came with a nice bonus. Then I remember that I'm going to have to buy a new house first. Alright, maybe not a big salary after all. But free accommodation and food should be a convincing argument. There may even be catnip cookies.

I push my plate away. "Is there dessert?"

"Glutton," Lily snickers but gets up to get a little chocolate pudding from the fridge. "High milk content. Just the way you like it."

I sigh in contentment as I take the first mouthful. Dark chocolate and milk, the best combination ever.

Now that I'm no longer as hungry, my brain is starting to work again. So much happened last night, so much we need to talk about.

"Where's K2?" I ask once I've finished my pudding.

"Sedated," Bethany mutters without looking up from her magazine. "We thought that was safest while

Gryphon was sleeping. She's with Benjamin, and yes, he's still sick."

"Maybe he'll pass on his bug to her," Four says gleefully. "That should make her weaker and easier to handle."

I exchange a look with Gryphon. "Did you tell them that she talked to me last night?"

"Briefly, but we were all tired. We should have a chat about everything that happened. Maybe it's best to wait until Lennox is back though. But first, show me your arm."

My arm? Ah. Yes. I almost forgot about it, mostly because it no longer hurts.

He carefully unwraps the bandage that I put on after the shower last night. I flinch when he removes the final bit, revealing the wound. It doesn't look pretty. It's closed, but it's not healed as much overnight as it should have. I think this is going to leave a thick scar. Whatever that poison was inhibited my shifter healing. Thank goodness for Ivy's licking ability to at least stop it from bleeding.

I give her a small smile. "Thanks for licking me."

"No problem." She grimaces. "It tasted awful though. Please don't get poisoned again; I can still taste it even now."

"Not planning on it. Bethany, did they tell you about the poison? Show you the antidote?"

She finally puts her magazine aside. "Yes, but it's nothing I've seen before. It seems to be a synthetic substance." She purses her lips as if personally offended by the idea of using poison that's not made from natural plants and minerals. "I'm going to try and produce more of the antidote, just in case. And once K2 is awake, we might want to try and take a sample of her claws."

"You think her claws produce the poison? I assumed she'd smeared it on them."

Bethany shrugs. "No idea. I no longer assume anything. The Pack scientists are doing things I never thought possible, so it's best to keep an open mind. For all I know, they've made poison drip from her claws, produced by her own body."

I shudder at the thought. As if K2 isn't damaged enough. "When is she going to wake up?"

"Hopefully the sedation is going to last a few more hours. Gryphon was exhausted; he needs a break from having to control her."

She gives me an accusing stare, as if that was my fault. Well, in a way, it was. I've dragged the guys into this. They may never have got mixed up in the Pack mess if they hadn't met me.

Gryphon gets up and returns moments later with a little jar. He puts the fruity-smelling salve on my scar, dabbing it so gently he's almost not touching it at all.

"I'll take another look at it later. Depending on what supplies Bethany has, I might be able to make something more effective to reduce the scarring as much as possible."

He expertly wraps the bandage back around the wound, hiding it from sight. Thank goodness. I hate being broken on the outside.

A scent hits my nose and I jump up. Wolves. I reach for my knives and realise I'm not wearing any. Fuck.

The door opens and Lennox strides in, followed by two unfamiliar men. Both wolves.

He grins, but it seems a little forced.

"Hi guys, I've brought some friends."

CHAPTER FOURTEEN

The taller of the men is in his late fifties, with grey streaks running through his black hair and wild beard that covers most of his face. His eyes are like glimmering coals, full of repressed power and authority. He's wearing a long leather coat that's frayed in places; it's clearly seen many battles. He's not carrying any obvious weapons, although I bet there's a knife or two hidden in his tall black boots.

The other guy is younger, maybe early thirties, and very broad. He reminds me of a barrel; short and thick. His eyes are a striking azure, the only colour in his otherwise bland attire. Thin scars line his face and neck like a spider's web. Curious. Shifters don't scar easily, so if they do, it's usually big scars that didn't heal well. Like the one on my arm. His scars are tiny, barely visible, making me wonder what caused them.

The older man extends a hand. "I'm Mr Moon, Lennox's employer."

I take it, not wanting to show my hesitation. I grew

up surrounded by wolf shifters, which is why I'm not a fan of them. Lennox excluded, obviously. "Kat Feln, owner of M.E.O.W. Pleased to meet you."

I'm amazed at my manners. This is Business-Kat, the persona I put on when I meet clients to discuss the assassinations they want to commission. I don't usually behave like this out of my office. The only problem is that I'm in nothing but a t-shirt and panties, with no trousers or even a bra. Not exactly professional, but Mr Moon hasn't even looked at my nakedness at all.

His grip is firm but not threatening. I wait for the other man to introduce himself, but he stays quiet. Alright then. A bodyguard, maybe?

"Apologies for interrupting your breakfast, but this cannot wait."

I nod. He should be sorry. "No worries, we were just finished." I wish I still had my office. I'd be a lot more comfortable talking to him there rather than in a messy living room slash kitchen in an old wagon. It doesn't feel very professional. Now that the final lab has been destroyed, I need to start looking for a new home for us. This place is starting to make me feel claustrophobic already.

"Let's go outside to talk," I say, but Lily gets up and nudges Bethany to do the same.

"We were just leaving, you can take our seats," she says pleasantly. At least she doesn't offer them tea. I don't want them to stay for long. We have a lot still to discuss, especially now that Lennox is back.

"Ivy, Four, come with me, I've got something to show you."

Mr Moon smiles at her and folds his large frame to fit onto the bench. The younger man joins him without a word. The two of them look totally out of place here.

The four girls leave, making the wagon feel slightly less cramped.

Lennox puts a hand on my lower back. "Morning," he whispers. "Sorry about this."

"Miss Feln, Lennox has told me about your encounter and I felt it was necessary to talk to you in person. Those wolves you met in the forest, tell me more about them."

"I didn't so much meet them as defend a helpless kitten from their attack," I correct. I turn to Lennox. "How much have you told them?"

He shrugs. "As much as I knew."

"Which is pretty much everything. I'm not sure I can add anything to that, Mr Moon."

He flashes me a smile, his eyes glinting. "I have a theory about what they are, but to confirm that, I need to know every little detail. You must tell me everything."

I sigh. "Why? I don't know anything about you. All wolves I know are either with the Pack or on the run from them. You seem to be neither."

Mr Moon looks at Lennox, pride reflecting on his bearded face. "So he's not told you. Well done, Lennox. I knew I could trust you." He turns back to me. "You were right about most wolves being with the Pack or on the run. I was part of them, a long time ago. I even believed in what they were doing was right."

I tense, but he holds up a hand. "That's in the past. I grew up in a feral pack of wolves. There was no order, no rules. It was carnage. We killed aimlessly, terrorising the local humans. Sometimes, we even killed each other. When I saw what the Pack was doing, I thought it was a better way. Controlling shifters, giving them purpose. It took me a while to realise the truth of it. That it wasn't for the benefit of us shifters at all."

"You know who's really in charge," Gryphon states.

Mr Moon nods. "I do. When I found out, I was furious. Since I was in a fairly high position in the Pack, I wasn't collared. I was there by choice. So I left. They tried to get me back, but I wasn't one of their cubs who went crazy being without a collar for the first time. I was a grown man who was stronger than most of them. In the end, they left me alone, and I created my own organisation. An alternative to the Pack, which provided the order and discipline needed to raise shifters, but without the collars, the experiments, the torture."

"That sounds too good to be true," I say honestly. "And how come I've never heard of you?"

"We work in the shadows. Everyone who joins us is sworn to secrecy. Breaking that oath is punishable by death. Which is why I'm very glad young Lennox hasn't told you about us. I would have hated to have to make an example of him."

Fuck. Now I wish I hadn't pressured Lennox to tell me about his employer. No wonder he was so adamant about not telling me. If he had, he would have been automatically sentenced to death. He should have told me, though. I would have understood. Probably.

Mr Moon clears his throat. "Back to the issue at hand. Lennox told me that the wolves you encountered had the same scent as the mutant bears the Pack has created. Is that right?"

I nod. "Are they really bears?"

"Human DNA spliced with that of a bear shifter they captured years ago," he confirms. "The only bear shifter I've ever encountered. Until then, I believed they were a myth. Well, the Pack caught him and experimented on him."

"No surprise there," Ryker mutters. "That's all they seem to do."

"You must, therefore, understand my concern," Mr Moon continues. "If they've somehow mixed bear shifters with wolves, I need to do something about it. I will not see my kind being experimented on."

"But it was fine when they did it to us cats?" I snap, suddenly angry. "You must have known about that if you were really as high up in the Pack as you say."

He meets my eyes and slowly inclines his head. "I knew. Fragments, not the whole picture. I saw you sometimes when you grew up. I knew you were different, that you weren't just a stray they'd caught. But there was only a tiny circle of people allowed to interact with you. All part of the experiment. Everything was monitored, every conversation with you recorded. And I had other things to worry about."

Yeah. Sure. There's always something more important.

"Mr Moon took me in," Lennox says quietly. "After I escaped the Pack, I was feral for a while. I was completely out of my mind for only a few hours, but I didn't regain full control of myself until weeks later. I wasn't as careful as I should have been. The Pack almost caught me, but Mr Moon helped me and offered me a new home."

"In return for working for him," I interject, still angry at the older wolf.

Lennox shrugs. "Yes, but it was my choice. I could have walked away and tried to survive on my own. I *chose* to stay. Without Mr Moon, I may never have lived long enough to see you again."

I'd love to counter that argument, but I stay quiet.

"Back to the issue at hand," Mr Moon says after clearing his throat. "I need to find those wolves and whoever created them."

I have to suppress a groan. This sounds like my own feline cloning situation all over again. I'm not going to investigate wolf cloning too. I like Lennox *despite* him being a wolf, not because of it. Cats and dogs will never be friends on the species level. Individuals, rarely. Lennox is an exception, mostly because he behaves like a cat half the time.

"Lennox and Ryker went to see the corpses after I killed them. I only defended a little kitten from them, that's all I did. I didn't really have time to worry about strange wolves afterwards; I've been kind of busy."

That's a complete understatement. Busy doesn't even cut it.

"By the time we got there, the bodies were gone," Lennox explains. "I never got the chance to tell you."

Ah yes, that's because when they came back, I was a mess, spilling my soul to Gryphon. I'd rather not linger on that memory. I'm Business-Kat now; there's no room for emotions.

"That means there were more of them, not just the three you killed," Mr Moon says, stating the obvious.

"Or maybe it wasn't other wolves but their creators," I reply. "I would have smelled it if more shifters had been nearby. I was on high alert and fully shifted. They would have had to be very far away to escape my notice."

He nods. "That would mean that either they had some sort of way of monitoring the wolves from afar, letting them know that they'd been killed, or that non-shifters were watching you without you realising. Sirens, maybe."

I shake my head. "Unlikely. I've been around sirens often enough to be able to recognise their scent. It might be quite similar to that of humans, but it's distinctive enough for me."

"There's a difference?" he asks, seeming genuinely surprised. "I didn't think there was. No wolf has ever been able to distinguish between a human and a siren, which is why it took me so long to realise who was really running the Pack."

Curious. Back at the Pack, I knew some people smelled different from others, but I didn't think much on it. Now, in retrospective, I know that even then I could tell sirens and humans apart, just without knowing what I was doing. If what Mr Moon says is true, he might not know that there's a siren in the room with us.

I exchange a look with Gryphon, who seems to be thinking the same thing. Let's hope the wolf won't find out. Gryphon is the ace in my sleeve that I don't want anyone to know about.

"Could you take me to where you fought the wolves?" Mr Moon asks pleasantly.

That guy really isn't giving up.

"I'm sorry, but-"

"I can give you something in return," he interrupts me. "You may not realise but news of last night's events has already spread. Don't worry, Lennox didn't say a thing. I have eyes and ears everywhere. I know you attacked one of the Pack's labs yesterday and I presume the reason for that is finding out more about Project Indigo?"

He knows the name of the fucking experiment? I could kill Lennox right now for not introducing me to the wolf before. We could have had some more answers before now.

I keep my expression blank. "You presume correctly."

"Then you will like my proposal. You help me find the wolves and I will help you retrieve the remaining clones. The ones held in the facility you haven't found yet."

CHAPTER FIFTEEN

I clutch the mug of tea, staring into the steam rising up from it. A lead has come to my door, my fricking door. And I almost didn't let it - him - in.

Mr Moon and his silent companion have left with the promise to return at twilight. He's assembling a team to help search for the mutant wolves. I'm not sure why he needs my help if he's already got a team of expert trackers, but oh well. He's offering me information on my sisters, so I'm all too willing to lend him my aid.

The twins returned as soon as he left the wagon. Not sure if they were listening in from the outside, but if they did, they've not commented on anything that we discussed. They're sipping on their mugs of hot chocolate that Bethany has made them. She's built a strange rapport with them. I think she turned into their hero when she gave them the cocoa; their expressions were priceless.

"Sorry about that," Lennox says for the third or

fourth time. "I only went to him to say that I'd be gone for a little while longer, but someone in our Pride found blood in the forest and I kind of blurted that I knew what that was all about."

"Your Pride?" Lily asks. "Isn't that what you call a group of lions?"

"Yes, but since the Pack already exists in this town, Mr Moon decided to steal that term and make it his own. Proud to be the Pride, that's his motto."

"Bah. I don't trust him." Four's voice is dripping with disgust. "He worked for them and knew what was happening. He could have stopped the experiments, yet he left and turned a blind eye."

"I agree," her sister mutters, staring into her cup. "Things could have been very different for us if he and people like him would have stood up and done something. He may think himself to be a good guy because he left and built a better organisation, but he's still a coward and a selfish bastard to me."

"Hear, hear." Four holds up her mug like a beer tankard. "Let's drink to that."

Lily chuckles. "Beth, did you put something in their cocoa?"

"I might have overdone it on the sugar," Bethany admits. "But they looked like they needed a little pick-me-up."

She's going to spoil them, I can see that already. Just like Benjamin spoils Ryker's cats, the kittens especially. I bet there are several of them on his bed just now, keeping him company while he's sleeping off his cold.

"Did someone check on Benjamin?" I ask the girls, reminding myself that I'm supposed to be a good employer.

"Yeah, he's getting better," Bethany says with a yawn. "And K2 is still out of it. We'll have to decide soon though if we want to keep her sedated or take the risk of letting her wake up."

"We can't keep her like that," I protest. "That's like something the Pack would do."

"Did you remember that she tortured me?" Ivy glares at me. "She's not safe to be around. She'll kill us all as soon as she gets a chance. Gryphon won't be able to control her forever."

"No, but we might be able to find a way to cure her," I respond, trying not to sound too harsh. Ivy is right to be afraid. K2 is unpredictable and seeing that she almost killed me, I should be scared as well. I'm not, though. All I feel for her is pity.

I sigh. "Let's talk about what happened last night. I'm missing a lot of what happened, just like you don't know what occurred between K2 and me. Who wants to start?"

"Me." Lennox grins. "I was hit by exploding brain." He sounds really happy about that. Is this the moment where I question my choice of boyfriend?

I smile at him. "I'd be more interested in the lead up to the brain exploding. What happened after I left?"

"He started being more cooperative as soon as Lennox returned with the collar," Four says with a cheeky grin. "Almost pleasant. But of course we weren't sure if he was telling the truth or not, so we put the collar on him despite his protests."

"He wasn't happy about that," her sister adds.

"Not at all. He did a lot of screaming and begging, but Lennox was great, he simply ignored him and put the collar around his neck. As soon as it clicked shut, the guy went all glassy-eyed and drooled on his shirt."

Ivy chuckles. "He looked hilarious. I really enjoyed that bit."

"So did I. After a minute or two, he kind of came round, looking a little more alert. He was able to answer questions, although he spoke in a bizarre and slow way. Like. This. Two words. At most." She giggles.

Oh my. My sisters are weird.

Luckily, Lennox takes over before I have to tell them to stop laughing.

"He told us that he wasn't part of the project at the very beginning, so you and K2 were already born when he became Professor Lakefield's assistant. He was assigned to her, but he also worked on a couple of experiments that involved you or other clones. Sisters, sorry. Some of the scientists focused on the behavioural side of the project, but he was more interested in the physiological. How he could change your behaviour with drugs rather than with the collar or by training you."

I lifted my mug to take another sip of tea, but it was empty. Oh well, I wasn't in the mood to get up and make more.

"Let me guess, he created the drug we were given? The one I found in the lab?"

Lennox nods. "It's one of several he experimented with. I don't know how many drugs you and the others were exposed to, but he led us to a filing cabinet that is supposed to have all the answers."

"Don't worry, we removed that before we set the building on fire," Four says with a wide grin. "It's hidden near the lab, waiting for us to collect. We would have carried it here, but then the cat came and told us that you were injured, so we didn't have the time. We carried it outside while Ivy played with her matches and hid it before following the cat."

"Thanks for prioritising me over some files."

She smiles as if I'd been serious. "You're welcome."

"That was when he'd started talking about the effect this drug had on K2," Lennox continues. "How it made her unable to shift while turning her more feral at the same time. But as Four said, then the cat came and we asked him for the antidote like the note instructed. He knew immediately what we were talking about. I bet he instructed K2 to poison you."

"And then his head blew off," Four interrupts. "Exploding into tiny bits. There wasn't as much blood as I expected, not until he fell down and it started squirting from his neck. You know, because there was no head to keep it in."

"Yes, thanks for the explanation, I know about anatomy," I quip. I can't help myself; I hate being patronised. I've decapitated more people in my life than most assassins ever will. I'm an expert decapitator.

Lennox chuckles. "So then we followed the cat until we got to you." His smile disappears. "You were unconscious and barely breathing. While I tried to make you drink the antidote, Ivy looked after your wound."

She licked it, he means. My sister licked my arm. Totally cat behaviour.

"When you were recovering, Gryphon told us to take Ryker home. The twins wanted to stay with you, but I wasn't sure if Ryker might not need Ivy's help, so we all went together. The rest is history."

He wanted Ivy to lick my Ryker. And she's already licked Gryphon. This is getting out of hand.

Lily gets up and puts the kettle on the stove. "Sounds like you had all the fun while we were bored out of our minds," she complains. "Next time, I'm insisting to be in on the action."

"Ryker's heart stopped, Gryphon's stomach was slashed open, Kat got injured and poisoned, and they were all almost gassed," Bethany summarises. "I think I'm rather happy I stayed home."

Lily shrugs. "When you say it like that..."

"Your turn, what did K2 tell you?" Four asks me, ignoring the two humans. I should really stop counting Lily as human, but she looks like it and besides her skill in seducing guys, it's not like she's very powerful. I'm so glad she can't read my mind just now; she'd kill me. She hates being seen as ordinary.

"First of all, you have to know that she was completely coherent," I start after Lily has refilled my mug. "Not like when she was behaving like a zombie or fighting us like a robot ninja. No, she was like a real person, with feelings and expressions and life."

"You're such a poet," Bethany snickers.

"Shut up. She told me that she sometimes had moments like that, when she was fully in control of her own mind, but that these moments were getting rarer." I fill them in on the rest of what K2 said, kind of regretting that Gryphon had been my only witness. The twins look as if they don't believe me. Or at least like they don't believe that K2 could have behaved in such a lucid way. I understand their side, of course. Ivy was tortured by K2 and they were both attacked by her several times. It's only natural for them to be cautious.

"Maybe we can find something about the siren net she mentioned in the files," Gryphon says once I've finished. "Who wants to come help me collect them? I'd rather not be here when the wolf shows up again."

"I'll come," Ryker, Ivy and Four say at once. I can't help but laugh. They all seem desperate not to have to deal with the wolves. I'm the same, but it's not like I have much of a choice. I just hope that it's worth it, that Mr Moon really has the information he says he has.

I check the time. "We still have a few hours until he comes back. By then, K2 will be awake. What shall we do with her? Gryphon, do you think you can control her?"

He frowns but then nods. "Yes, but only while I'm awake. I hate to say this, but I agree with sedating her while I'm asleep. It's safer for all of us this way, until we've found a solution. But if we can wake her up now, I'll sit with her for a bit and see if I can experiment a little with how best to control her.

Uh oh. That sounds dangerous. "Want some company?"

He shakes his head. "It'll be easier to focus if I'm not distracted by you wearing my shirt. But if you hear me scream, please come and save me. You can even do it without a shirt."

The twins start giggling while I imagine how nice it would be to disappear into thin air.

CHAPTER SIXTEEN

Dusk comes sooner than I would like. I'm snuggled against Lennox's chest, breathing in his scent. We're in the living room, so I can't touch him in the way I want, but it's better than nothing. I've changed into my usual black attire. Sadly it's not my favourite leather suit; that needs a lot of repairing, if it can be saved at all.

I feel a lot more comfortable having my knives in all their usual places, plus some poison darts and a garrotte. You never know who you may have to suffocate.

Gryphon, Ryker and the twins left as soon as the sun disappeared beyond the horizon. I doubt they'll be back until the wolves have left again. Benjamin is still in bed, as is K2, now sedated again. I never got to see her while she was awake; Gryphon spent several hours trying to figure out a way to reach her mind without letting go of his control over her. He's not had any luck yet, but as frustrated as he seemed, he's not given up hope yet. And who knows, we might find something helpful in the files they're retrieving.

Lennox stiffens behind me. "They're coming."

I extend my senses but can't hear or smell anything. "How do you know?"

"It's a wolf thing."

Well, that doesn't explain anything, but I let it slide. We have more important things to do tonight. Like finding some mutant wolves so that Mr Moon can tell me where my remaining siblings are.

It takes another five minutes for him and his companions to arrive. Instead of letting them into my wagon, we wait for them outside. I don't need wolf stink all over my furniture. Lennox is the only one allowed to mark this home with his scent, and even then, I'm glad that us cats are in the majority.

"Miss Feln, I'm glad you didn't change your mind," Mr Moon says instead of a greeting. He's got five wolves with him, all of them clad in black and all of them very, very big. It's like he only allows the strongest wolves to join his Pride, or maybe the others are at his home, doing the less exciting work.

"Are you ready to go?"

I nod. "Let's do this."

"First, I'd like you to lead us to where you fought the wolves. I know most traces will be gone by now, but we might find something other people would overlook."

I try not to roll my eyes. Sure, let's go on a wild wolf chase through the woods. A group of testosterone-filled shifters with me as the only feline. What could possibly go wrong?

Three of them shift into their wolf bodies, but Mr

Moon stays human. He smiles pleasantly. "Lead the way."

* * * * * *

By the time we reach the forest, darkness has taken over. Even to me, a creature of the night, the woods in the dark are a creepy place. It's taken us ages to get here. I hadn't realised it was this far. Last time, I was a panther filled with adrenaline from a fight. Being human is making me slow.

Mr Moon hasn't tried to initiate a conversation, and I don't feel like talking to Lennox while having an audience, so we walk in silence. The wolf hasn't introduced his companions, but I don't really care. After tonight, I'll never see them again.

When we get closer to where the wolves had cornered the kitten, I extend my senses, sniffing the air, listening to the sounds of the forest. Many animals have passed through here since and the faint smell of rain predict that no traces will be left for us to find.

I easily recognise the place, even in the dark. And just like I told Mr Moon, there's nothing left to see. Wet leaves cover the ground where I left the bodies of the mutant shifters.

"Spread out, search the area," he commands nonetheless. I stay close to Lennox, watching as the wolves get to work. The ones who've shifted walk around with their noses close to the ground, while those who haven't inspect the trees and lift rocks. Stupid, if you ask me, but nobody does.

After a while of watching his men work, Mr Moon steps into the centre of the crime scene. His dark eyes start to glow red, like lit coals, as he slowly turns in a circle. This must be some kind of creepy wolf thing I don't know about.

"What is he doing?" I whisper to Lennox, but my wolf is frozen in place, his eyes fixed on Mr Moon. They're glowing a little too, not as much as the older shifter's, but enough to freak me out. "Lennox?"

He doesn't react, doesn't even blink. Fuck. What kind of magic is this? None of the wolves is moving; they all seem to be in some sort of trance. I've never seen anything like it, not even at the Pack which was full of wolf shifters. I thought I knew everything there is to know about them. Seems I was very wrong.

I step over to Mr Moon, waving my hand in his face. "What the fuck are you doing?"

"Silence," he growls without looking at me.

I won't let him shut me up. He's got my friend, my mate, under some kind of mind control. I won't allow that.

In one fluid motion, I draw a knife and hold it to his throat. The steel glints in the night, a familiar sight that eases my worry somewhat. Most things can be solved with a blade and determination.

"Let him go," I hiss, baring my teeth. I feel my incisors grow into fangs as I glare at him.

He doesn't respond, doesn't even flinch. I press the knife closer against his skin until I draw blood.

"Stop," he groans, suddenly sounding exhausted

even though his expression doesn't change. "Just a bit more."

A bit more what? Time? Blood? My mate's life energy? I listen out for Lennox's heartbeat just to make sure he's alright. It's a little faster than it should be, but nothing dangerous.

"One more minute, then I'll cut your throat," I announce, but I lessen the pressure a little. I don't want him to injure himself accidentally if he makes any sudden moves. I don't like Mr Moon but I'm intelligent enough to know that killing him would get me into deep trouble. He's powerful. Besides, Lennox might be a little upset if I killed his boss.

I count the seconds, readying myself to make good on my threat, but just before the time is up, Mr Moon's eyes stop glowing and he steps back, his shoulders slumping and his breathing heavy. He looks as if he's just battled a pack of rabid dogs or run a marathon.

"Kat."

I swirl around and run to Lennox. He's leaning against a tree trunk, looking just as exhausted as his employer.

"What the hell just happened?" I demand. "You scared the shit out of me."

"Sorry, I didn't know he was about to do that," he huffs, holding his side. "Or I would have warned you. Gosh, I forgot how rubbish I always feel afterwards."

"After what?"

"The Linking," Mr Moon explains, no longer sounding as boisterous as before. "It's a practice not known to many. I'm probably the only wolf in this town who knows the technique. The Pack certainly don't, or they would do all sorts of evil with it."

"But what is it?"

"We connect our minds to extend our awareness and find echoes that we may not see otherwise. Echoes of consciousness, traces of whoever's been in this place. It only works for other wolves and I was doubtful whether the mutants were still wolf enough, but luckily, they are."

I'm flabbergasted. Echoes of consciousness? That sounds like a load of hogwash.

Lennox takes my hand. "I know you're about to attack him, but please don't. He's speaking the truth."

"I wasn't," I mutter, but I'm not quite sure. Mr Moon is irritating me and I don't think I'll be able to control myself in his company for much longer.

"We saw the wolves," Lennox continues and I stare at him in surprise. "It's hard to explain, but imagine it like shadows. They're gone but their shadows are still here, lasting longer than any scent ever could. You ripped out two of their throats and sliced open the other's belly, am I correct?"

I nod, slowly. The taste of the wolves' blood fills my mouth, a sweet memory that should repulse me. Well, my mind finds it disgusting, but my body is betraying me. My saliva glands go into overdrive and I have to swallow, forcing myself to think of something else.

"We didn't see you in the Linking, but we did see them die. They lay here for a while, and then they were carried away. Not by wolves though. Again, we couldn't see whoever it was who moved them."

"Which means we're looking for either humans, sirens or something else entirely," Mr Moon says loudly, sounding more like himself again. The other wolves are gathering around him, all looking a little worse for wear. I wonder if he warned them before he did the Linking. I feel like it's something that consent should be given for.

"Sir, I saw something." A wiry man steps forward, his white goatee shining like a light in the darkness.

"Yes, Jake?"

"It may be nothing, but there was a shimmer, like the one I told you about before."

Mr Moon sighs. "Which turned out to be irrelevant."

"But what if it is?" Jake asks defiantly.

He sighs again, even more dramatically this time. "Alright, tell me exactly what you saw. Where was this shimmer?"

Jack walks a few steps towards a large tree. I remember jumping past that just before I ripped out the first wolf's throat. Once again, I smell his blood on my tongue. I tighten my hands into fists, squeezing my fingernails into my skin. The pain makes me focus.

"It was here. The shape of a woman, slim, small, long hair. I couldn't see her features. She looked at the wolves and watched as they were being carried away. She's powerful. That's why I could see her. She was in charge, I'm sure of it."

"A mysterious woman in charge of the mutants," Mr Moon mutters. He doesn't sound convinced. "Anyone else got something? Any traces? Scents?"

Nobody replies. His team is either really bad or

there isn't anything to find. I'm very tempted to say 'told you so', but that wouldn't work with the professional persona I'm trying to keep up. Not that it's working; the knife-against-his-throat wasn't my usual business style at all. I like to threaten and intimidate, but not with a blade and definitely not when I want something from the other person. Let's hope he forgets that little episode.

"Jack, can you follow the shimmer?" He says the last word with distaste.

Jack nods. "For a bit, but I'll need some more of the Linking or I won't be strong enough."

"We can't do that again," Mr Moon says vehemently. "It's taken too much of a toll on everyone already. Is there no other way you can do your voodoo?"

"Not voodoo," Jack complains. "I'm just a little more sensitive to some stimuli than others."

Mr Moon rolls his eyes as if he's had this conversation before.

"It might help to have someone touch me who's seen the mutants. Who's touched them."

Ehm, is he talking about me?

"No touching," Lennox growls, suddenly beside me, pushing my back so that he's in front of me.

Down, doggo. But I don't say that. I don't want to embarrass him in front of the other wolves. I may let him act all alpha and macho now, but he's got something coming once we're back home. I'm going to show him exactly who's boss. Heat blossoms in my core at the thought. Yes, he's going to be put in his place.

"I need to touch her, it's necessary," Jack argues. "She's killed the wolves and therefore their traces are on her. If I can get a good read of her memories, I might be able to track the woman."

"Wait, you're going to look at my memories?" I push past Lennox and stare down Jack. "No way."

He bows his head, even though he seems surprised about it. I guess he's not used to showing subservience to people who're not part of their Pride. Least of all cats. "Not memories as such, miss, just...imagine it like footprints. I can't see the man who left it, but I can estimate his size and weight. It's like that, except that it isn't."

"Jack is our resident philosopher," Mr Moon groans. "Half of what he says doesn't make any sense, but occasionally, he's right about it and has a brilliant idea that helps us. It's why I keep him around."

Footprints. Shimmers. Linking. My head is swirling with all those strange concepts. And here I thought that this was a just a simple tracking exercise. I wish I was back home in the warm wagon with a cup of hot chocolate, a catnip cookie and one or more warm bodies to lean against. At least I have Lennox here with me. I step back until I'm pressed against him, as if by accident. He doesn't react - well, most of him doesn't. I repress a smile. Someone's happy to touch me.

Which brings me back to the issue at hand. "So you can't see my memories?" I ask just to confirm.

"No, your secrets are safe with me." Jack grins at me, his goatee twisting strangely as he does. How very comforting.

"I guess I don't have a choice then." I stretch out a hand. "Here you go, that's as much as you get to touch.

Please hurry up, I've got better things to do than being...touched."

Lennox snickers softly, just loud enough for me to hear.

Jack carefully takes my hand between his, as if he's scared I'll gut him if he does anything more. Which he's right about. My other hand is at my waist, close to the hilt of my dagger. If he does a wrong move, I'll have his throat cut before he can even open his mouth to apologise.

"Close your eyes, please, and remember what happened here," he says, his voice suddenly a lot deeper and calmer. I do as he says, but I don't relax. Closing my eyes doesn't mean I ignore all my other senses. I'm still on high alert, even if I may not look like it to the outside world.

"Think of when you arrived. You were here for the cat, right? Was it injured?"

"*She* was being attacked. Cornered by three wolves."

"You don't have to say it out loud," he mutters. "Just remember, picture it in as much detail as you can."

Alright then. What a weird thing to do.

The kitten's meows. The wolves, rabid, saliva flying from their mouths. Their claws, sharp, reflecting the morning sun. The smell of the leaves as I run towards them. The wind tousling my fur. The first bite, the blood. So sweet that I couldn't help myself.

"That's good, very good," Jack whispers. "Keep going."

The first wolf, dead on the ground. The second, jumping high above me, then organs raining down on me. More blood. The third wolf, me on his back, my teeth around his neck. Another kill. More blood. Then the kitten, meowing in shock.

"Gotcha. Boss, you're not going to like this."

I open my eyes as soon as Jack lets go of my hand.

"Why, what is it?" Mr Moon asks, his voice serious.

"It's her. The Hypnotisse."

CHAPTER SEVENTEEN

Lennox and I are waiting for an explanation, but Mr Moon isn't in any state to give it. He's fighting his shift, brought on by the anger blazing in his dark eyes. Black fur is erupting from his skin and his fingernails are curving into claws. He's close to the point of no return, but he's strong. He might make it without the whole shift.

Everyone's stepped back and is watching from a safe distance. Getting close to a shifter trying to control himself is never a good idea. In the midst of the shift, we're vulnerable, which makes our instincts go into overdrive. If he suddenly thought that was one of us is a threat, he'd complete the shift and be at our throats before we'd even know we were his prey.

"Do you have any idea what this is all about?" I whisper to Lennox, keeping my body language completely calm while Mr Moon groans and shakes.

"Not the faintest. I didn't even know Jack could do this. I've not been very active in the Pride recently though, as you may have noticed." He grins at me. "I've had more exciting things to do." He lowers his voice even further. "Some of them are saying I shouldn't come back at all. I stink of cat, apparently."

"Well, if they throw you out, you know where your real home is. Once we have a proper home again, I mean."

He squeezes my hand. "Let's see how the future will turn out."

I'm a little sad that he didn't tell me right away that of course, he'd move into the new house. That he'd stay with me rather than return to his Pride. I guess it's a wolf thing. They like being around their own kind, far more than us cats do. We tolerate each other, and families do have certain bonds, but what Ryker has done - creating an entire feline community - is highly unusual.

Slowly, Mr Moon is getting calmer and his fur recedes. His eyes are still glowing, but that seems to be almost normal for him. He's a strange man, I give him that.

I stifle a yawn. The last few days have been exhausting. Make that the last few weeks. I could do with a holiday. Maybe that's what we should do. Travel to different cities, explore them until we find one we like, then buy a house there. A holiday with house shopping included. I bet Lily would love me forever; she adores travelling. Not sure about the others. Except for Gryphon, we're all from this town or at least the area. But what is really binding me to this place? Nothing. On the contrary, once the Pack is completely destroyed and I no longer have to worry about other shifters being in danger or my sisters being tortured, then I'll be completely free. A new town might be just what I need. A new beginning. No baggage. Just me and my family and a suitcase full of cash.

"You look happy," Lennox mutters. "Care to share the joy?"

"Later," I promise. "I think your boss is about to be fully back to normal. Let's solve this puzzle so we can save my sisters."

That's what this is all for. My sisters. Not that I don't care about wolves but... yeah, I don't really care. They're just glorified dogs who lift a leg to piss and don't have their tails under control.

Mr Moon straightens his frayed coat and runs a hand through his wild mane, then comes over to where Lennox and I are waiting. He doesn't apologise for being a little feral.

"Have you heard of her?" he asks without preamble. "The Hypnotisse?"

I shake my head. "No. Is that even a word?"

He growls softly. "It's what she calls herself, even back at the Pack. She's one of them. A siren. Their most powerful weapon. I've never met a more deranged woman in all my life, and that says a lot." He laughs. "You should have met my ex. She was crazy as fuck."

I barely manage not to roll my eyes. I have no interest in his love life. For all I care, he could be rutting with ten naked virgins each night while drinking blood. No, let's not keep that image in my head.

"So she's a siren?" I ask and his reminiscent smile disappears.

"That she is. Strong, as I said. She could control even us shifters without having to try hard. And she loved it."

"Sounds like a true siren," Lennox mutters. "They do love forcing others to do their bidding."

"She was very...unstable," Mr Moon continues. "When I first met her, I thought she was a teenager going through a very wild puberty, but she was already in her early twenties then. Her mood swings were the cause of countless deaths. When she was unhappy, people had to suffer. At the same time, whenever she was happy, folks around her would go into a strange state of ecstasy, dancing and kissing and taking off their clothes. I kept my distance from her, and pitied the ones tasked to look after her."

"Why would anyone let her run around free if she had that effect?" I ask. "It's not like the sirens have any problem with incarcerating people and experimenting on them."

Mr Moon smirks. "She's the daughter of the most high-ranking siren in the whole region. That made her untouchable. Besides, her mother is a little crazy herself, so I doubt she ever realised the whole extent of her daughter's madness. Anyway, when the Hypnotisse reached her mid-twenties, someone suggested she take on a project. It was basically meant to keep her busy and stop her from killing Pack members, but it backfired. She started experimenting on sirens and shifters alike. I don't know any details, but from what I heard, she made Project Indigo sound like a lovely wellness experience. She might be the most dangerous woman I've ever met because she hides her intelligence behind the facade of madness. I think she has more control of herself than she lets everyone believe." He sighs deeply. "And now she's mixed up in wolf business. I guess it's time to face her and bring her to justice."

Mr Moon is such an arrogant dick. He didn't care while she was doing terrible things to other people, but now that wolves are affected, he suddenly wants to act. Pathetic.

Lennox clears his throat to get his boss's attention. "Do you still need us? It's getting a little frosty."

"No, you run off, I'll be in touch when we can use your assistance. Lennox, we will need to have a chat soon about your future. Miss Feln, I'll contact you tomorrow with the information you require about Project Indigo."

I give him a short nod and turn away, glad to be out of here. I can still taste the blood in my mouth and I hate how much I crave it. If a mutant wolf came across us now, I wouldn't be able to stop myself from gorging myself on his blood."

I suck.

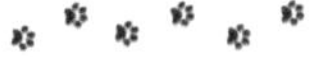

RYKER AND GRYPHON ARE ALREADY IN BED BY THE TIME we make it home. They're still awake though, talking, but they stop as soon as we enter the wagon. Secrets? I shall have to find out. I love a good mystery, especially if it involves me.

Someone has left a plate of sandwiches on the table. How very thoughtful. They deserve a pay rise. I snatch the only salmon one and take it into the bedroom, happily munching on the smoked fish. It helps distract me from the echo of blood in my mouth. I hope this is going to end soon; I can't continue like this. I'm starting to feel like a vampire.

I let myself fall onto the bed, right between the two guys. Lennox disappears into the bathroom, giving me a moment alone with them.

"How did it go?" Ryker asks. "You stink of wolf."

"Urgh, tell me about it. Next time, I'm taking you with me as back up. Far too many dogs in one place. It reminded me of the Pack, except that there was a lot more testosterone."

Ryker laughs. "Did they mark any trees on the way there?"

Gryphon snickers. "You two should hear yourselves. If I didn't know better, I'd say your racist. Dogist. Wolfist?"

I throw a pillow at him, almost losing hold of my sandwich. "Oi! I'm a very tolerant person, but I'm a cat at heart and my instincts are telling me that wolves can't be trusted."

"With exceptions," Lennox shouts from the bathroom.

"Of course!" I yell back. I wouldn't have needed to; his hearing is good enough to hear whatever we're talking about.

Gryphon sits up and wraps around me from behind, his head on my shoulder. "I think you smell of the forest. I like it."

"You're blessed with your inadequate nose," Ryker grumbles. "You don't have to imagine how they were all over her."

"Nobody was on me. I shook Mr Moon's hand and one of his wolves touched my-"

Ryker growls, his yellow eyes flashing in anger. "He did what?"

"-my hand," I complete the sentence, amused at his reaction. "What did you think? The only wolf allowed to touch more than that is Lennox."

"Thank goodness!" he shouts from the shower. I need to tell him that it's rude to eavesdrop. But then, I would have done exactly the same, obviously.

"Why did he do that though?" Gryphon asks. He shifts his position, rubbing against me. And then he takes a bite from my sandwich. That little devil! Here I was, thinking he wanted to cuddle when all he was after was my precious salmon.

"I'm not going to tell you now." I pout. "That was theft."

Gryphon chuckles and kisses the back of my neck. "What can I say, I'm an excellent thief. But since I made those sandwiches, it's not really theft at all. You took one without asking so you're the one in the wrong."

"Wait, you made them? I didn't know you could cook."

"It's not what I'd call cooking. I cut a few slices of bread and threw stuff on them."

Yeah, okay, he makes it sound easy. It isn't. Making sandwiches is extremely difficult. I never manage to get the toppings onto the bread without eating them straight away.

"Would you hurry up eating that so I can kiss you?" Ryker complains.

"No kissing before I'm back!" Lennox calls out.

"Do I get a say in this?" I ask, still practising my pout.

"Nope. But maybe get a shower too, I don't want to kiss someone smelling of wolf." Ryker grins innocently. "I'd be happy to help you shower, by the way. You know, to make sure all their scent is gone."

"We need a bigger bathroom," Gryphon sighs. "And a bigger bed. And a bigger everything."

I let them bicker while enjoying my sandwich. When I'm done, I'm still a little hungry. I could have needed that bite Gryphon took from me. As a punishment, he's not going to take part in the shower.

I take Ryker's hand. "Shower time."

CHAPTER EIGHTEEN

I wake up draped across Ryker with one hand each on Gryphon and Lennox's chest. Even in my sleep, I claim them all.

The room smells of sex. There's a tiny window at the top of the wall, but I can't be bothered to get up and open it. Ryker is nice and warm and I love the way his chest moves whenever he breathes, pushing me up and down like a wave.

I close my eyes again. I'm no longer tired, but I'm comfy and happy in this position. There's no need to get up before I really have to. Snoozing is a wonderful thing.

Staying in bed until everyone's woken up naturally, then a lazy breakfast with lots of milk, then lounging outside in the sun, doing absolutely nothing.

A knock on the front door makes me sit up.

I shouldn't even have dreamed of a quiet morning. Those don't happen to people like me.

I extend my senses. Nobody else is home who could open the door. Not even K2. Damn.

Wait, no K2. Fuck.

I jump up and grab a random shirt from the floor. Gryphon's, this time. How is it that they always bury my own clothes underneath theirs? Not that I care. I run out of the room, through the living room and into the second bedroom where K2 was last time I checked. Empty. Her scent still lingers in the air, as does Benjamin's. He was too ill to leave the room yesterday, so he either recovered really quickly or they were taken.

"What's going on?" Lennox yells from the other end of the wagon.

I don't answer and hurry to the front door. Unsurprisingly, it's Mr Moon. Bad timing.

"Not right now," I tell him and shut the door again before running back to the bedroom.

"Gryphon, did you sedate K2 last night?"

"Bethany did, yes. Why?"

"She's gone."

That makes him sit up fast. "Gone?"

"Nobody else is here. It's just us." Panic creeps into my voice.

"Could the humans have taken her for a walk?" Ryker asks, sounding worried.

Gryphon shakes his head. "No way. She only walked when I told her to. She must have woken up from sedation earlier than planned. Maybe the Pack sirens somehow took control of her again."

He gets up and puts on clothes as fast as possible. I realise I'm only in a t-shirt and quickly do the same. If K2 has kidnapped the M.E.O.W. team, we need to search the area.

How the hell did this happen? I don't usually sleep this deep. I never shut off like that, I always keep aware of what happens around me even when I sleep. Except for last night. I've become complacent. Fuck. This is bad. I'm losing myself. Maybe being with the guys is a bad idea. It's distracting me from being the person I need to be.

"I'm going to talk to my cats, maybe they saw something," Ryker announces and hurries out of the room while whistling loudly, his trademark call to his cats.

"Ask them to get the twins," I shout after him. I'm sure he's got his cats watching them. I have no idea where they stay when they're not with us, but Ryker wouldn't be Ryker if he didn't have his spies follow them.

Lennox doesn't bother putting on more than sweatpants. "I'll deal with Mr Moon. If K2 is out on the streets, he ought to know too."

"Tell him that she mustn't be harmed," I warn him.

He nods. "Of course."

In that moment, I love him to bits. He doesn't question me wanting to protect a woman who's a danger to this town. He just accepts it.

I know myself that this may be the end of the line for K2. If she gets into trouble, I might be too late to save her. And if she's on the way back to the Pack or some other sirens, it will be hard to get her out of there. I wish we'd had more time to work on freeing her from their control, but with everything else going on, including the stupid wolf problem, there just hasn't been the opportunity. Guilt rises up in my throat like acid. I should have prioritised my sister over a random pack of wolves. Yes, Mr Moon promised me information on my other sisters, but that could have been a ruse. K2 was right here, with me, yet I ignored her.

Gods, I'm an awful big sister to have.

With Ryker and Lennox away, I turn to Gryphon. "Is there any way you can find her? You've connected to her, but I don't know about siren stuff so I have no idea, but..."

He wraps me in his arms. "Don't worry, we'll find her."

"We don't need to," Ryker calls from outside. "I know where she is."

WE FOLLOW THE CAT, A TINY LITTLE THING WITH WHITE legs and a permanent scowl, through the outskirts of town where our wagon is based. She's said it's not far, but she's refused to tell us anything else. I don't like her. This might be the first time ever I've been tempted to torture one of my own. Her silence frustrates me to no end.

Ryker is holding my hand, squeezing gently from time to time. My tension lessens for a moment whenever he does it, before crashing back into me a second later.

Lennox has stayed back to deal with Mr Moon, but Gryphon is next to me. Even though he's not holding my hand like Ryker, he's close, his shoulder bumping into mine every few steps. I appreciate how he's trying not to overpower me with his touch while still being there, showing that he's here for me. That's how I interpret it, anyway. Maybe he just likes bumping into me.

The cat meows when we reach a narrow alleyway sneaking its way through two rows of tall buildings. It's not the nicest part of town but there are worse. Another cat, this one a male, jumps from a metal bin and meows in greeting. They rub noses. Their love is evident even for those who can't speak their language. So cute. But not what I should be focusing on just now.

"Where is she?" I ask impatiently.

The male cat turns to me. His whiskers are pure white, while the rest of him is mottled in all sorts of colours. Like an artist emptied his leftover paints all over the cat's fur. Gorgeous in a chaotic kind of way.

He doesn't meow, but I can read his intentions nonetheless. He wants me to be quiet and follow him. I translate for Gryphon, the only one in our group not able to communicate with the cats.

He nods, not finding it strange at all to take orders from a feline. I guess he's used to it by now. For someone who's not a shifter, he blends in remarkably well. Maybe it's a siren skill. They do need to blend in to pull the strings from the background. It's why nobody knows about them. They could be anyone.

We sneak down the alley, where an old archway leads towards the river. Grass grows on top of the red bricks that threaten to collapse in the next big storm. The two cats stop before we can duck underneath the archway, and the male extends his paw to point at the scene before us.

I suck in a breath. K2 sits on the banks of the river, her trouser legs rolled up to her thighs, her feet dangling in the water. Bethany is next to her, amicably chatting with my sister. Who shouldn't be supposed to be able to talk. Nor look as relaxed as this. Lily is standing halfway across the river, laughing as tiny waves crash against her naked legs. The only one missing is Benjamin.

"What. The. Fuck," Gryphon mutters before I can do it.

This is the complete opposite of what I expected. Hell, I could never have anticipated this at all. From afar, the three girls seem like the best of friends who're enjoying a day by the river, cooling off from the non-existent heat. I wouldn't be surprised if they brought a picnic.

The male cat meows and Ryker translates. "They've been here for about an hour. The cats thought it was a little strange but they didn't want to disturb us." He rolls his eyes. "You don't want to know what they call what we did."

"I do, actually," Gryphon retorts.

Now that we know K2 and the others are safe, the tension has lifted. I can breathe again. And laugh.

The laughter springs from my mouth before I can stop myself. I laugh and laugh, holding my belly, tears springing to my eyes. The guys look at me, a little confused at first, then they join my hysterical laughter. I sense the cats' confusion, which makes me laugh even harder. This must be the strangest situation I've ever found myself in.

K2 turns around and waves at us. Fricking waves.

As if this was the most normal thing ever. As if she hadn't begged me to kill her just two days ago. I think my mind is blown. I need a drink, or some catnip, or both.

I walk towards them, taking my time, still a little scared to startle my sister. I mean, she almost killed me, I'm allowed to be a little hesitant around her. Bethany finally realises that we're here and turns, giving me a cheeky grin.

"Sorry, we thought about waking you, but you seemed like you needed sleep."

"You were very loud last night," Lily states while wading through the water towards us. "I can't wait to be in a house again where I'm far away from your bedroom."

Had I been noisy? I don't remember. It's all a bit of a blur. Lots of touching, kissing and orgasms.

"Sorry," Ryker says, surprising me. "It's still new to me, doing this as a human. So much more intense."

"Alright, back to the elephant in the room," I snap before they can continue talking about my sex life. "What the hell are you doing?"

"Caitlin wanted to see the area," Bethany replies with an innocent smile. "Since the weather is nice, we decided to go to the river. Benjamin was feeling well enough to go to the pharmacy by himself. He might join us later on."

"Elephant. In. The. Room." I have a hard time not

shouting at them. Why isn't anyone telling me what's going on?

"It was supposed to be a surprise." Lily steps out of the river and sits down on the grass, rubbing her legs. Her skin is bright red; the water must be freezing. "We solved it last night while you were out befriending the local wolves. Bethany wanted to tell you, but I thought it would be much more fun to make it a surprise."

"I'm going to skewer you and stuff you into fortune cookies if you don't tell me right now," I growl. "Then you can be a surprise for all the people I'm going to feed you to."

She laughs. Urgh. Can't she at least pretend to be scared?

"You're adorable when you're angry. Why don't you sit with us and we can explain it all?"

"Yes, sit." K2 hasn't said anything until now. Her voice is far more relaxed than I remember.

It seems I'm not getting anywhere at all. I flop to the ground, cross my legs, and glare at the girls. Lily giggles as I shoot daggers at her. Just metaphorical ones, sadly. I won't kill her until I've got my answers.

"Tell. Me."

I grind out the words, barely managing to keep a hold on my temper.

Gryphon sits down next to me and puts a hand on my thigh. If that is supposed to calm me down, it's not working. Ryker stays standing, the two cats at his feet, watching us with bemused expressions. I guess life is a lot simpler for them.

Bethany sighs theatrically. "Alright then. Last night,

I gave Caitlin the usual sedative, but I mixed it with something else. You know how I've been trying to replicate the drug they gave you? Well, after you brought home some of it from the lab, I compared it to my own poor attempts. Not having my own laboratory hasn't made it easy, but I think it's a testament to my skills that I've managed to synthesise a version of it."

"A version?" Gryphon asks. "Why would you want more of the stuff?"

"I didn't create the same," Bethany corrects herself. "I made the opposite."

"An antidote?"

"No, an antidote would stop or reverse the effects of the drug. I've created something that does exactly the opposite. While the original drug separates your connection with your feline side, my version increases it. Why, you ask? It's because I'm a genius."

I roll my eyes. "A little less self-importance, please."

"You're boring. My theory was that Caitlin was able to be controlled so easily by the sirens is because they increased her human side. Sirens have a much harder time controlling shifters, right, Gryphon?"

He nods. "It's possible but only for the strongest of us. I can only influence Kat to an extent. I can lead her into a direction, but if I tried to make her do something that she was really opposed to, I'd fail. I wouldn't be able to make a shifter harm themselves or others, but I could do it to a human."

"That's exactly what I was relying on," Bethany says jubilantly. "By giving her my new drug, I made her less human. I don't think I'll ever be able to reverse the separation they caused, but it seemed to be enough for their control to slip. When Caitlin woke up, she was able to talk to me. It was slow, at first, but she managed to fight off the sirens' control and stay herself."

"It's easy now," K2 confirms. "I still feel their presence, far in the back of my mind, but they're weak. Even if this is a one-off, I'm going to enjoy it."

She turns back to the water and moves her feet around. I wonder if she's ever done this before. Sat by a river, carefree and without any obligations. Free.

"What's with the name?" I ask gently.

"You asked me whether I had one. After I talked to you, I was still mostly conscious. I wasn't as gone as I had been before. I was able to think. So I decided I wanted a name. By the time Bethany woke me, I knew which one I wanted."

"It's a pretty name." I don't tell her about the other Caitlin I knew once, the girl who worked in Mr Kindler's sweet shop. Who was responsible for shifter children being killed. Who was killed by Gryphon. Better to let her start with a blank slate.

I turn to Lily and Bethany and give them both a glare. "Do you have any idea how worried we were when you weren't at home? We thought something had happened to you. That you'd been kidnapped or goodness knows what."

"Stop sounding like my mother," Lily scoffs. "It was just a surprise."

"You thought I took them," Caitlin says quietly without looking at me. "And I understand that. But I need you to know that I'm no longer K2. I have my life back. I don't know if it's going to last, but I don't want to live in K2's shadow. She's done horrible things, but I haven't."

"We've got company," Ryker suddenly says.

I sniff the air. Oh my. Double trouble is about to arrive.

The twins aren't happy. They stare at Caitlin as if she's about to grow a second head just so she can devour them both at the same time. It's clear they don't trust her.

"She should be locked up!" Four shouts at me. "Not running around, free to kill whoever she wants."

I hold up my hands, trying to calm her. "It's safe. Look at her. Look into her eyes. She's no longer controlled by the Pack. This is the real Caitlin now."

"Caitlin?" Four spits. "She's given herself a name. That doesn't stop her from being a monster. She's playing you, and you don't even notice because you're trying to see the good in people. Wake up, Kat. She's not who she pretends to be. The sirens are still controlling her."

"I know you're scared," Caitlin says gently, surprising all of us. "But you don't need to be. I'm sorry for what K2 did to you. I'm sorry I look like her. But I'm not sorry for being me. For being alive."

This is becoming increasingly confusing.

Ivy steps forward. "Do you remember hurting me?"

Caitlin's eyes widen as she takes in her sister. "Fragments. Whenever they made me do bad things, I tried to hide. So many bad memories... I couldn't do anything to stop it. My body moved without me having control. You must believe me, I never aimed to hurt you. Especially not after I found out who you were. They told me, after. They laughed about it. How I'd almost killed my own sibling."

"Did they call her a sibling?" Gryphon asks.

She frowns, confused. "No. A clone. They called all of you clones."

He smiles at her. "But you decided to see them as siblings." He turns to the twins. "The proof is in the little details. She wouldn't decide to claim you as her sisters if she was out to hurt you. That wouldn't make any sense. She'd try and distance herself from you so that she wouldn't have to feel guilty. And if it's any help, I can no longer feel the siren influence on her. Last time, I could barely reach her mind because they fought me for it, but this time, it's completely different."

"Try and make her do something," Four snaps. "Prove that she's no longer under your or any other siren's control."

Gryphon's smile disappears. "That would be against the rules I live by."

"Do it, please," Caitlin asks softly. "If it helps them understand. Just...don't make me kill anyone."

He sighs. "Alright. And I won't."

Gryphon starts to hum, the same gentle melody I've

heard him use before. It's not one of his battle songs nor the raging melody of love that he's used on me. It's simple but elegant. I let the music wash over me, immediately feeling lighter. Caitlin gets up and stands on her tiptoes. I frown at Gryphon questioningly, but he just smiles and continues his song.

Caitlin starts to dance. Wow. She moves like air, almost seeming to float on the grass. She turns and jumps and pirouettes and does all sorts of moves that I don't have names for. But the best thing is her smile. I've rarely seen anyone this happy. A deep, base happiness that transcends everything else.

I steal a glance at the twins. Both of them are gaping at our sister, their mouths slightly parted, their eyes wide. They've never looked more alike.

Gryphon's melody changes slightly and suddenly, Four's arm twitches, before both her arms stretch up, her hands meeting in the middle in an elegant arch. She starts to dance as well, moving away from her sister, joining Caitlin.

Alright, I have no idea what's going on here. What is Gryphon up to?

Ivy is still in the same position, but now a smile is curling her lips as she's watching her sisters.

"If they can dance like that, does that mean you have the same moves?" Ryker whispers.

"Don't even continue that thought," I hiss. "I'm not going to dance."

He wiggles his eyebrows in the way I like. Naughty boy. He knows I'm having trouble resisting him when he does that. "Just in theory. Could you dance?"

"Not even in theory. This conversation is over."

I turn away from him despite the pretty wiggling eyebrows. His charm only goes so far. I'm not going to dance for him. I wouldn't even know how, unless my fighting moves can count as dancing. I guess I can do the dance of death, but I need my knives for that plus a victim who I can kill at the end of it. Dancing is no fun without a little blood.

Gryphon's melody is becoming slower and so are my sisters' movements. By the time the final note springs from his lips, they're standing opposite each other, breathing hard. Four has her eyes closed, but now she slowly opens them, blinking into the daylight. They look at each other. I wish I could read their thoughts.

An unspoken conversation seems to pass between them, then Four inclines her head.

"Hey, sister."

Caitlin smiles. "Hey."

I think my heart is about to explode with a strange, overwhelming feeling. I adore these girls. No, wrong word. But I'm not going to use the other one. Not yet. I don't want to commit myself. Yes, they're my sisters, but just because we share the same genetics doesn't mean we need to lo…adore each other. For now, I'm aiming for none of us killing one of the others. That seems like a good start.

"Explain what just happened," Ryker demands, turning to Gryphon. "I thought you weren't supposed to control them?"

The siren grins. "I didn't. I just gave them a little push."

"Wait, so you didn't make them dance?"

"I gave them a suggestion. They could have easily fought it, but they both accepted it as an order they wanted to follow. Probably because I wasn't asking them to do anything bad. I took them by surprise."

"Did they already know how to dance?" I ask him. "Or did you show them how to?"

"My sister used to take dance lessons. I had to come along sometimes when the babysitter was ill." His expression turns grave. "I didn't realise back then, but now I know what the bruises on her face meant. My father never liked the babysitter, but my mum did, so she stayed. Well, she was ill a lot."

Gryphon's father sounds like a real arsehole. I'm going to enjoy taking him down, eventually. He's quite far down my list but one day, I'm going to work my way through the list and deal with all the people who've hurt my family and fellow shifters.

Ivy walks up to us, smiling happily. "Thank you. I've never seen Four so relaxed. I think she needed this."

Gryphon returns her smile. "She needed almost no encouragement at all. It was like she craved the excuse to just let go. You though, you fought me. Why?"

She shrugs. "I grew up in very different circumstances from Four."

That doesn't explain anything, but I don't pressure her to continue. We all have our secrets. Our pasts.

The male cat comes over and rubs against Gryphon's legs, meowing loudly.

Ryker laughs. "He wants you to teach him how to dance. I think you've just got yourself a new job."

Gryphon stares at the cat. Then hums a cheerful melody. And the cat begins to dance.

CHAPTER TWENTY

Lennox and Mr Moon are waiting for us in the wagon's living area. I'd hoped the wolf would have left by now, but at the same time, I need the information he's promised. My sisters have stayed by the river, with some cats watching them to make sure they don't get into trouble. Ryker complained that we're now using his cats not just as spies, but as babysitters too, but I know that deep inside, he loves getting his feline family involved. Ever since he learned to shift, he's not spent as much time with them as he used to. He must feel guilty about that. I'll need to have a chat with him on what to do with the cats when we move.

"Everything alright?" Lennox asks.

I'm not sure if Mr Moon is aware of the situation, so I just nod. "Everything's under control. And here?"

Mr Moon puts down his mug. Lennox has made tea for them, but the distinct smell of hot whisky betrays the wolf. Tea and whisky? Not the combination I'd choose, but each to their own.

"I'm glad you came back, I was just about to leave."

"Have you made any progress on your wolf problem?" I ask.

"Not yet, but I have been given information suggesting that the Hypnotisse has left town and is operating from somewhere else. That would explain why we've not come across any of these mutant wolves before. I've got my best people on it, so hopefully, we'll know where she's hiding soon. Once we do, will you join us in fighting her?"

I smile in what I hope is a non-committal way. "Let us know once you have more information. But now, I think it's time you hold up your end of the bargain."

He nods, his expression going grave. "Do you have something to write?"

Ryker hands him a piece of paper and a pencil. Mr Moon scribbles down a few words. An address.

"This is where you'll find them. And I'm sorry."

I tense up. "Sorry for what?"

"I'm sorry," he repeats and gets up. "For your loss."

THE ADDRESS IS A WAREHOUSE IN THE NORTH OF TOWN. We reach it in record time, even though we circled town to avoid being spotted. I shifted as soon as Mr Moon said those words, with Ryker and Lennox doing the same. We left Gryphon behind, but I'm sure he understands that I couldn't wait. He's slow, he'd hold us back, and I need to know what happened to my siblings.

Gravel crunches beneath my paws as I approach the

warehouse. It's a fairly new building but it looks abandoned.

"Can you sense anyone?" I ask Ryker.

"No, I don't think there's anyone here. Maybe they left when the Pack leaders were killed. My cats say the Pack is disbanding; their headquarters are almost empty."

The news that we've finally managed to destroy the Pack should make me happy, but a sense of dread has taken hold of me. Mr Moon's words echo in my head. *I'm sorry.*

No signs of life. That means that either this building only contains a clue to my sisters' whereabouts or… no, I'm not going to continue that thought. I need to focus on the present. One step at a time.

The warehouse has two large double doors big enough for carts to fit through, with a smaller door to the side. I press down the handle with my large paw. It's locked.

I exchange a look with Lennox and without a word, he shifts back to human. It makes sense for him to do it; I can communicate with Ryker while shifted but not with the wolf. Now that he's human, we'll be able to understand his words.

He takes forever to pick the lock. I have to stop myself from shouting at him to hurry up. He's doing his best, I know that. It's just so hard to stay patient.

Finally, the door opens with a click. I storm inside, pushing past Lennox and Ryker. The warehouse is one large hall with a small office on one side, separated from the rest with tall glass windows. The shelves in the office are empty and the desk is bare. Dust plays in the light streaming in from skylights.

A few old wooden crates are stacked at the other end of the warehouse, with some of them looking close to falling apart. I doubt they're storing anything valuable in there. Probably just stuff they couldn't be bothered to remove. Opposite are strange metal lockers with square doors. That's all that remains in the otherwise empty hall. No sign or any people, least of all my sisters.

Mr Moon's information must be out of date. The trail has gone cold.

Deflated, I head to the little office and shift. I stretch, arching my back, before starting to look through drawers, hoping they forgot some important documents that might tell me where my siblings are. I know I'm deluding myself, but I can't give up hope just yet.

The guys are exploring the rest of the warehouse. Ryker has shifted as well and is taking apart the wooden crates, spilling their contents on the dusty floor. Batteries, tins of food, blank paper, strange metal tools. Lennox inspects the metal lockers.

I turn away from them. They'll call me if they find anything interesting.

A few staples and pins are all I find in the drawers. The bin hasn't been emptied, but it's just boring bills for the rent and electricity of this place. Nothing that helps me. I kick the desk in frustration.

This is useless. The trail has grown cold and we're back where we started.

"Kat!"

Lennox's voice is strange. Detached. Without emotion.

I walk towards him, slowly. The dread curling in my stomach is getting stronger. He's opened one of the locker doors. His shoulders are drooped, his expression grave.

Deep inside, I already know what he's about to say.

Ryker cuts me off before I reach the lockers. He takes me into his arms, stopping me from going any further. His body is a barrier that I can't accept. I fight against his grip, but he holds me tight, ignoring my struggles.

"I'm so sorry," he whispers.

I cling to him with one hand while I scratch him with the other. I need to see. Need to know.

Lennox closes the locker door, but the movement shifts the air, bringing the scent I've been dreading right into my nose. So familiar. Even in death, they still smell like me.

The wolf joins us and hugs me from behind. I'm sandwiched between their warm bodies, yet all I feel is cold.

"Both of them?" I ask, my voice breaking.

"Yes. I'm sorry." Lennox's breath is warm against my neck.

A strange numbness takes over. It's not just my body that's cold. It's my mind too. My thoughts turn sluggish.

"Breathe, Kat."

I don't. I scream.

* * * * * *

THEY NEVER STOP HOLDING ME. EVEN WHEN I SINK TO the floor, unable to keep standing. Even when I rock back and forth. Their hands stroke my back, my hair, whispering words that never reach me. I'm empty inside. Something has been ripped from me, something so precious it can never be returned.

Gryphon joins us. He sings to me, but this time, his song does nothing. It's just a hollow melody. Just as hollow as I am.

"I need to see them."

I've said that before.

"No," Lennox whispers. He's done that before, too.

We're going in circles of pain. I want to cry, but I can't. No tears reach my eyes. My chest hurts. My heart is breaking, shattering into pieces. Eight of them. Eight versions of me. Three of them gone. Four found. One far away.

A cat snuggles against my legs. Black with a golden stripe on her forehead. Shara. Mila's girlfriend. Mila was killed by the Pack. As were my sisters.

I reach out to her and run my fingers through her soft fur. She understands my pain. Shara meows softly and rubs her head against my hand. She meows softly. *I know.* I can almost hear her voice in my head. *I feel it too.*

That's what breaks me. Finally, the tears come. Wet and salty, hot and painful.

The guys hold me even closer. A whimper escapes my lips. And another.

"It's okay, just let go," Ryker whispers. "We're here."

More tears. They run down my face and drip onto

my shirt, creating a wet patch. Usually, that happens with blood. Did my sisters bleed? Did they suffer?

"How?" I ask, choking on the question.

Lennox strokes my hair. "They look peaceful. No injuries. As if they're sleeping." His voice breaks.

"We need to get them home. Somewhere warm. It's so cold here."

"Of course. We'll give them a proper burial," Lennox promises. "Let's get you home first."

I shake my head. "I can't. I need to see them."

"No."

"He's right," Ryker whispers. "It won't help."

A sob breaks over me like an icy wave. I can't do this. Can't sit here being surrounded by my men while they're over there, alone and cold in a locker.

I push them away as hard as I can and scramble to my feet.

I need to see.

CHAPTER TWENTY-ONE

TWO WEEKS LATER

Little Kat squeals in delight as Aunt Rose puts the cake in front of her. Seven candles. In between, tiny cream roses. I'm tempted to reach out and swipe one of them up. I can't wait to start eating. Hurry up.

My sister takes a deep breath and blows out the candles. One of them flickers, fighting hard, but then it expires. Little Kat grins widely and wipes away the smoke with her hands.

"Happy birthday," Aunt Rose cheers. "Many happy returns."

"Happy birthday," I echo, as do the others.

It's the first time we're all together. Caitlin, the twins, Little Kat and me. Five sisters, united at last. Behind me are the guys, watching with amused smiles on their faces, while Lily, Bethany and Benjamin are outside, preparing the barbecue.

Gryphon's sister is in the kitchen with her boyfriend.

The two of them are adorable, but they keep to themselves. Young love and all that. I'm going to have to have a word with them later though. Little Kat told me of how she was curious about the sounds coming from their room at night, and how she's planning to investigate. It almost made me choke on my punch. Little Kat may not have had the best childhood, but I'm definitely going to try and preserve her innocence for as long as possible.

She proudly cuts the cake into massive pieces - ignoring the advice of Aunt Rose - and takes the biggest piece for herself. Good girl. She no longer looks as starved as when I first found her and she's grown quite a bit. Her hair is glossy now and her skin radiant. I can't thank Gryphon's aunt enough for what she's done for my little sister.

Little Kat is young enough to still have a future. She's started going to school and while she has trouble interacting with the other children, I'm sure she'll get there eventually. The one thing that she's still not changed is her name. The kids at school call her LK, Rose has told me, which I guess isn't too bad. Maybe she'll come up with her own name eventually. Like Caitlin.

The oldest of my siblings stands a little removed from the rest of us, watching with a smile. I take two plates of cake and join her, handing her one of them.

"Thanks. It looks delicious."

"Trust me, everything that Aunt Rose makes is amazing," I tell her, remembering the homemade ice cream she gave us the first time I visited. "Little Kat has been raving about her pancakes. I was kind of hoping we might get them for dessert today."

"I've never had pancakes."

And just like that, my mood drops. She's sixteen and has never had pancakes. In all her life. How I hate the Pack. Not that I ever got any when I was living with them, but I had the freedom to go to street stalls and get some there. Lennox and I would sneak off and either steal or buy sweets with the few coins we sometimes managed to hold back. Of course, our Pack handlers would have beaten us blue and black if they'd found out that we didn't give them all the money we had, but it was worth it. My mouth waters as I remember the warm cinnamon buns we once stole by climbing through a bakery window. They were totally worth having the baker running after us, shouting and cursing.

"If we don't get any today, I'll make some for you," I promise. "Or even better, go to a cafe and have proper ones. I might set the kitchen on fire if I try it."

She laughs softly. "I've been told that it wouldn't be your first time."

"Hey, that wasn't entirely my fault. Well, maybe it was, but people should really stop gossiping about my culinary skills."

"Or absence of skills." Lily joins us, smelling of smoke. "How's the cake?"

Before I can tell her that I've not had a chance to try it yet, she steals my fork.

"Yummy," she moans, "we have to come here again. Or make Aunt Rose our official M.E.O.W. cook. I'd donate ten percent of my salary to employ her."

I snicker. "How very generous of you. But Rose might like to stay here. She's got her daughters and Gryphon's sister living with her. And Little Kat, of course."

I watch the youngest member of our family as she munches on her cake, her face covered in icing. She's so adorable that I'm having a hard time not running across the room to give her a long, hard cuddle. It's not going to be easy leaving her here. Who knows when we'll be able to visit.

"Have you told her yet?" Lily asks.

I shake my head. "No, but Rose knows. She's okay with keeping Little Kat. In fact, she threatened to use her siren powers on me if I had any intentions of taking the girl from her." I laugh at the memory. "She's quite formidable. I think Little Kat will be safe here, now that the Pack is dispersed."

Ryker's cats have combed the town to look for remaining shifters, but found none. The Pack members who weren't killed by us must have left. We set their headquarters alight after making sure that nobody was still there. Lennox says that Mr Moon has rescued several younger Pack shifters and taken them in. They'll be part of the Pride now. We're going to have to keep an eye on Moon. I wouldn't want his Pride to evolve into a new Pack. Lennox trusts him, but I don't, not a bit.

When he told me where to find K9 and K10, he knew they were dead, but never said anything. He tricked me and I hate him for it.

We said goodbye to my two youngest sisters last week. After some debate, we gave them a traditional river cremation. Cats don't bury their dead and in the Pack, bodies disappeared and were never seen again. Sirens have some kind of strange song ritual that requires at least ten of them, so we couldn't do that either. In the end, we did what the humans do.

It was beautiful, in a way. We laid them on small floats covered in phoenix flowers. Their bodies were wrapped in colourful fabric - and no, my men forbade me to ever look at them. It was hard not to, and I still regret that I didn't, but at the same time, I know that they'd haunt my nightmares even more if I'd looked.

When the floats were halfway down the river, I shot flaming arrows into them, alighting the phoenix flowers. Golden flames engulfed the floats, rising high up into the sky like the feathers of a bird.

The others left once the floats had disappeared in the waves of the rivers, but my sisters and I stayed there, looking out over the water. Caitlin, Ivy, Four and me. After the weird dance incident, the twins had decided to trust their older sister. She still takes Bethany's drug every day, just in case, and Gryphon monitors her vulnerability to his siren influence. I guess we'll never be a hundred percent sure that she won't be able to fall prey to the sirens again, but it would surprise me. Caitlin is strong, even though she's soft-spoken and a little timid. The killer persona she was forced to take on has nothing to do with the real Caitlin who is now peeling back the layers of years of torture and conditioning. She's beautiful inside. So much more innocent than me and the twins. I have no idea how she managed to stay this way, but I kind of envy her. With a bit of help, she might be able to start a new life, one without violence.

The twins are quite the opposite. They crave action and revenge. They want me to let them be part of M.E.O.W., but I'm not sure about that. They're too young to become assassins. I want them to get an education, have a childhood, learn to play. They wouldn't be able to do that if they stay with me.

"I've decided to come with you," Caitlin says, as if she's read my mind. "I don't want to stay in this town. Too many bad memories, even though I was mostly just in the one building. I want to be with you, help you find a new home, and then I will think about whether I'll stay or travel a bit. I want to see the world."

I take her hand, completely going against my usual way of dealing with emotions. I don't hug her though, I'm not that changed yet.

"You're welcome to stay for as long as you want."

"Thank you." She gives me a genuine smile. "I'm glad you found me. And that you didn't kill me."

"Yeah, me too." I laugh. "And I'm glad you didn't kill me either."

"We're a strange family. Being grateful for not killing each other. I wonder if other people have those conversations too."

Lily snickers. "Not my family, and we are all a little crazy. We do fight occasionally, but there are never any weapons involved."

I gape at her. "Not even a small blade? Like a kitchen knife?"

"Nope."

"Poisons?"

She shakes her head.

"Then what do you do for fun?"

Lily sighs. "Kat, you've got a lot to learn. I'm going to show you the joys of going out at night and playing seduction bingo."

"What's that?" Caitlin asks curiously.

"You make a list of what kind of people you seduce, like someone really hairy, someone wearing green shoes, someone exactly the same height as yourself. Then you have one night to tick off as many as you can."

Caitlin's eyes widen. She's so cute and innocent. "Do you sleep with them all?"

Lily shrugs. "If you want to, but it's not necessary. Proper seduction isn't all about sex."

"Don't talk to my little sister about sex," I groan. "I'm already going to have to have a word with Ryker's sister about that."

"You want to have sex with Ryker's sister?" Lily laughs loudly.

Urgh. Family can be so annoying.

I'M IN LOVE WITH AUNT ROSE. TRUE, HOT, PASSIONATE love.

This potato salad is amazing and I'm not even a big fan of potatoes.

"You're amazing," I tell her while chewing on a piece of crispy bacon. Yes, she puts bacon in her salad. Did I say that I love her?

"People keep telling me that," she says with a satisfied smile. "It's why my daughters still come over for dinner even though they're all grown up now. Although one of them has just moved to Attenburgh, so she won't be here for a while."

Attenburgh. The place where K7 is being held. The only one of my sibling who still needs saving. We know that for sure now. We've gone through most of the documents from the lab detailing Project Indigo. Only nine of us survived longer than past the first year. Of those nine, six of us are still alive.

"Is it a nice town?" I ask innocently.

"Oh yes. I lived there myself for a few years after I finished my studies. It's where I met my husband, actually." Her smile wavers but she continues. "It's much richer than here. Lots of very pretty houses. Pretty people. Not so pretty secrets. If you love gossiping, Attenburgh is the place to be. Every year, the siren high society meets there for their annual charity ball. Not that any of the money raised actually goes to charity, but whoever came up with the name thought it sounded nice. Much better than 'ball where everyone gets drunk and behaves badly'. I never much liked those events, but the town is lovely. Three rivers surround it, separating the richer areas from the slums outside."

"So I guess the house prices are high?"

She laughs. "Thinking of entering the property market?"

"Something like that."

"Well, yes, they are. You'd probably get a small flat there when you'd get an entire house here for the same price. You're in luck though. Guess where my daughter is working?"

I shrug. I don't know anything about her daughters. "A morgue?"

"An estate agent. I'll give Gryphon her address. I'm sure she can help you find somewhere that isn't too expensive."

I nod my thanks and nibble on a sausage while thinking it over. I'd planned to go to Attenburgh for K7 anyway, but now that I know that lots of sirens live there... I'm sure they'll have a connection to the Fangs. Or to the Pack. Either or, they're bad news.

Going there is a bad idea.

Which is exactly why I'm going to do it.

EPILOGUE

F our very fat horses are attached to the wagon, ready to pull it to our new home.

They lazily munch on hay while they wait for us to say our goodbyes.

Ryker is surrounded by dozens of cats. About half of his family has decided to stay here. He's leaving them in the capable paws of Storm. I'm sad she's staying, but she's the purrfect leader for his clan.

The other cats are already in or on the wagon. Little Pumpkin, Ryker's son, is on one of the horses. I'm surprised it hasn't thrown him off yet, but he's the kind of kitten who makes friends with everyone, including horses.

We said goodbye to Little Kat and Aunt Rose yesterday, so now it's just the twins who're here with us. It took me hours upon hours to convince them not to come with us. They're staying with Rose for the next six months. That's the most I've been able to bargain. After that, they'll be allowed to reconsider whether they want to come join me or stay here.

Rose has promised to find them a tutor. I have no idea if they've ever had any schooling, so they might have to start at scratch. Not that I'm educated or anything, but dealing with M.E.O.W. business has made me realise how important it is to know your way around numbers. Not that I'm grooming them to become my assistants and look after the admin side of things. Not at all. Liar.

They stand side by side, their hands clasped. I hate having to leave them, but it's best for them.

Even though they behave like grown ups, they are still children. I can't look after them by myself, especially not while searching for our remaining sister.

I clear my throat, completely at a loss to as what to say. I don't do goodbyes. I run and never look back. This is a first. Well, a second if you count yesterday when I had to say goodbye to Little Kat and Aunt Rose. At least Little Kat is too young to understand the concept of time. For her, if I see her again in half a year's time, it might feel like we only just met yesterday. That's what I hope, anyway.

"Look after yourselves," I say helplessly. "Don't get in trouble. Try not to kill anyone. If you do, hide the body. Acid works well for that. And if you get poisoned, give me a call and I'll put Bethany on the case. I'll send Aunt Rose my number and address as soon as we've found a house. And if you get stabbed-"

Gryphon puts an arm around my shoulders. I'm so flustered that I didn't even hear him approach.

"What she means to say is that you should take care and be good. And that we'll miss you. Right, Kat?"

I nod. "Exactly that. I meant the thing about the acid, though."

Ivy laughs. "Thanks. We'll call you if we have any bodies to hide."

"You bet." Four grins. "And don't get into trouble either now that you don't have Ivy to lick you."

Gross.

I give them a quick hug before hurrying to the wagon. I don't want them to see me this unsure of myself. I hate social interaction. I might just shift and curl up on the roof of the wagon for a bit, pretending to be a cat who doesn't have to deal with people.

Just before I enter the wagon, Four calls me from afar. "Hey, Kat! What does M.E.O.W. really stand for?"

I grin. "Haven't you figured that out yet?"

M.E.O.W.

Murder eases our worries.

The End

Meow! The story continues in Lick, the fifth book in the series. To get updates about the Catnip Assassins and other books, subscribe to my newsletter.

Kat would also like to encourage you to leave a review. Don't tempt her to sharpen her knives. She's scary that way.

Dear readers,

I can't believe that I've just completed Kat's fourth book. Originally, I'd only planned there to be three (well, it was supposed to be a standalone at the very beginning, but as soon as I got to know Kat, I realised that wouldn't be possible), but now there will be seven in total. That's right, three more Catnip books!

You can blame Debbie Cassidy for that, my friend and co-author. I was starting to talk about doing a fifth book for Kat because there's still so much story to tell, and she basically told me to make it into a new three-book story arch. So if you were hoping for this to be the last book (I hope you weren't), then blame her.

Now that the Pack is destroyed (finally!), Kat and her family will start a new life in a new town, but of course that doesn't mean that everything will be easy... far from it. There will be more assassinations, pawsome spies and even a diamond heist.

It's strange how Kat has become such an important

part of my life. I've been writing books about her for over nine months now. I'm currently drinking from a M.E.O.W. mug. I have two t-shirts featuring Kat and M.E.O.W. (all available at my Redbubble shop). And there's even a Kat chibi magnet on my fridge. If I'm not careful, I'm going to dress as Kat at my next book signing….

I hope you will continue following Kat's journey, despite the body count. I apologise to all vegetarians and vegans who found her blood frenzies a little overpowering (sorry, Renée!). And yes, I admit I had to cry a little when writing chapter 20. I would have liked to write something more positive but Kat had other plans.

Anyway, time to start writing Lick…

Lots of furry hugs,

Skye

ABOUT THE AUTHOR

Skye MacKinnon is a USA Today & International Bestselling Author whose books are filled with strong heroines who don't have to choose.

She embraces her Scottishness with fantastical Scottish settings and a dash of mythology, no matter if she's writing about Celtic gods, cat shifters, or the streets of Edinburgh.

When she's not typing away at her favourite cafe, Skye loves dried mango, as much exotic tea as she can squeeze into her cupboards, and being covered in pet hair by her two bunnies, Emma and Darwin.

Support her on Patreon and get exclusive benefits:
patreon.com/skyemackinnon

Subscribe to her newsletter:
skyemackinnon.com/newsletter

facebook.com/skyemackinnonauthor

twitter.com/skye_mackinnon

instagram.com/skyemackinnonauthor

bookbub.com/authors/skye-mackinnon

goodreads.com/SkyeMacKinnon

amazon.com/author/skye_mackinnon